THE SKILL OF SNOOPING

THE SIDEKICK'S SURVIVAL GUIDE, BOOK 5

CHRISTY BARRITT

River Heights

COMPLETE BOOK LIST

Squeaky Clean Mysteries:

Storm of Doubt

Winds of Danger

Rains of Remorse

Lantern Beach P.D.

On the Lookout

Attempt to Locate

First Degree Murder

Dead on Arrival

Plan of Action

Lantern Beach Escape

Afterglow (a novelette)

Lantern Beach Blackout

Dark Water

Safe Harbor

Ripple Effect

Rising Tide

Crime á la Mode

Deadman's Float

Milkshake Up

Bomb Pop Threat

Banana Split Personalities (coming soon)

The Sidekick's Survival Guide

The Art of Eavesdropping

The Perks of Meddling

The Exercise of Interfering

The Practice of Prying

The Skill of Snooping

The Craft of Being Covert

Carolina Moon Series

Home Before Dark

Gone By Dark

Wait Until Dark

Light the Dark

Taken By Dark

Suburban Sleuth Mysteries:

Death of the Couch Potato's Wife

Fog Lake Suspense:

Edge of Peril

Margin of Error

Brink of Danger

Line of Duty

Cape Thomas Series:

Dubiosity

Disillusioned

Distorted

Standalone Romantic Mystery:

The Good Girl

Suspense:

Imperfect

The Wrecking

Sweet Christmas Novella:

Home to Chestnut Grove

Standalone Romantic-Suspense:

Keeping Guard

The Last Target

Race Against Time

Ricochet

Key Witness

Lifeline

High-Stakes Holiday Reunion

Desperate Measures

Hidden Agenda

Mountain Hideaway

Dark Harbor

Shadow of Suspicion

The Baby Assignment

The Cradle Conspiracy

Trained to Defend

Mountain Survival (coming soon)

Nonfiction:

Characters in the Kitchen

Changed: True Stories of Finding God through Christian Music (out of print)

The Novel in Me: The Beginner's Guide to Writing and Publishing a Novel (out of print)

CHAPTER ONE

"THIS PAST WEEKEND WAS GREAT."

Michael Straley's voice sounded cozy as his gaze captured mine and swept me away to a place where nothing else existed—just him and me.

He tugged me around the corner—and out of sight from any watchful eyes—before we reached the sidewalk leading to our office building. As I leaned against the wood-sided wall, he stepped closer.

Michael's warm brown eyes were filled with affection that turned my blood into hot fruit sludge. It might sound gross, but the dish was a Yerbian delicacy. I'd grown up in the South American country, and I'd been craving the tasty dessert lately.

I rested my hand on his chest as I happily conceded. "It *was* a great weekend."

The two of us had not only coached a local softball team for a win, but we'd also found a murderer and had decided to explore a relationship between us.

On top of that, seven days had passed and the infamous Beltway Killer had not claimed a new victim yet in the area.

The serial killer had left a rose with a nautical knot around it last week at the baseball dugout at our practice field. In the past that had indicated that, within seven days, the Beltway Killer would strike again. The rose and the knot usually signaled who might be his next target.

Ever since I'd found the rose, I'd kept my eyes open for trouble. But I was okay, as well as my family and all the women associated with the softball team.

It looked like that rose and knot were either a falsely planted clue or that the police were wrong in their assumptions about why it had been left. Either way, I wasn't complaining.

In fact, I was now ready for a new week and a new case.

Brighter things were on the horizon. I could feel new opportunities inching closer, like a caterpillar headed toward chrysalis.

"We should get inside," I murmured, realizing I could stay here all day and be content.

Michael and I had already grabbed a quick cup of coffee together to start our day. As we'd sipped on our brews, we talked about our favorite foods, made plans for the next weekend, and brainstormed a project his seven-year-old daughter, Chloe, was working on for school.

Michael didn't seem in a hurry to get to work either, but he finally shrugged. "I guess we should go. If you insist."

"If I had a choice, I'd stay here until my legs collapsed like a xate tree with a treehouse on top."

"A what?"

"It's a Yerbian—"

"—expression," Michael finished. "I'm starting to catch on."

I grinned. "It's about time."

Michael quickly planted a kiss on my lips. Warmth spread through me at his touch.

I could really get used to this switch from friends to more than friends. Things just felt comfortable around Michael. Natural. Meant to be.

As he backed away, I tried to compose myself. With one more glance at each other, we strode toward the office. No one knew yet that Michael and I were dating, and we wanted to keep things quiet for a little while longer. We didn't know how our boss, Oscar Driscoll, would feel about this, and that pressure would just add one more complication to our relationship.

Michael and I needed to figure a few things out before we took that next step and told people. Plus, I *did* have some reservations about dating a coworker. I'd done it before, and the results had been disastrous. I'd be wise to remember the lessons I'd learned.

Michael took my hand and led me around the building. I willed my heart to slow at his touch, but it didn't work. Michael's touch caused a fire to rush through me.

That was a true fact, as Michael liked to say.

He released his grip as soon as we stepped onto the sidewalk.

"I wonder what's on the agenda for this week," I said, trying to use my most professional tone. But my voice cracked, rendering my efforts useless.

"Who knows? Could be a wayward spouse. An insurance claim. A stolen necklace. That's what makes this job interesting. It's something new every day."

As we stepped into the office of Driscoll and Associates, the private investigation firm we worked for, I opened my mouth to call hello to Velma, as I always did. She was our receptionist, administrative assistant, and resident extreme cheapskate.

I paused when I saw her empty desk.

She must have run to the bathroom.

I shrugged it off and went into my office, depositing my purse near my desk. At any minute, I expected Velma to appear and Oscar to open his door and bellow out some instructions. The man was a former police detective and acted like a dictator most of the time.

The man might officially be in charge, but he mostly let other people do his grunt work for him while he watched soap operas and ate pistachios. Occasionally, he rubbed elbows with the "elites" in town, which possibly drummed up business. The effectiveness of that was still to be determined.

As if Oscar had read my mind, his door opened. But this time, he didn't yell for us. Instead Oscar, with his out-of-date mustache and forty extra pounds, stepped out into the reception area.

He frowned as he glanced at Michael then me. "I thought you two were Velma."

The first trickle of concern washed through my system. "You mean she's not here?"

"I haven't seen her. It's not like her to be late."

Oscar was right. Velma seemed to really love her job and to take it seriously. She was always here when we needed her. She brought in muffins—mostly found discarded, but sealed for freshness, in dumpsters. She brightened the office with roses her neighbor had thrown out after a breakup. Recently, she'd taken to splitting our two-ply into one-ply to save Oscar some money—not that he'd asked her to save money.

Despite her quirky ways, Velma was a total asset to our team.

"Has anyone tried to call her?" I moved in front of my desk so I could read Oscar's expression.

"I'll do that now," Oscar said. "I was giving her a few minutes, in case she was stuck in traffic or something."

I paced toward Oscar's office and lingered in the doorway, listening as he picked up his cell phone and put it to his ear.

After a few minutes, he lowered the device and frowned. "No answer."

Michael appeared beside me and crossed his muscular arms over his chest, obscuring his "Watch for Glitches" T-shirt. "I wonder what's going on."

"Let's give her a few more minutes." Oscar sat down at his massive, throne-like desk. "I'm sure she has a *bona fide* explanation for this."

I might be able to justify that if Velma was just late. But the fact that she hadn't called and wasn't answering her phone ratcheted my concern up another level.

"While we wait . . . do you have any cases lined up this week?" Michael asked Oscar, stepping farther into his office.

"There are just a few minor things that we have going on." Oscar grabbed a handful of pistachios and leaned back. "We're going to be running some background checks and things like that. Nothing too strenuous."

I supposed that was a good thing, although those tasks were rather boring. I actually preferred doing fieldwork, something that surprised even me. Up until a month ago, I'd thought I was a list-making, number-crunching kind of girl. But maybe not.

At twenty-seven, I was still discovering new sides of myself.

"Why don't you guys take it easy for a few minutes?" Oscar popped more nuts into his mouth. "Velma usually goes through all my messages for me so I can sort out my week. As soon as she gets in, I'll have a little *tête-à-tête* with her and then we'll have our Monday morning meeting."

Velma pretty much did everything for him.

We all did.

I nodded and walked back into my office, the one that I shared with Michael. But as I sat at my desk, I realized I couldn't focus. My thoughts kept going back to Velma. I expected her to walk through the front door at any minute with some crazy story about traffic or breaking her heel or finding some kind of great deal in the garbage bin behind the bakery.

I tapped my finger against the desk and tried to turn my thoughts to something else.

"Have you heard anything from Grayson?" I asked Michael, trying to keep my mind occupied.

Michael twirled his chair toward me, a preoccupied look in his eyes. "I know he got to go home from the hospital. I planned on checking in with him later today."

At least there was that bit of good news. We'd asked

Michael's friend Grayson, who was CIA, to try to open an encrypted jump drive for us that my deceased father had left. But, in the process, Grayson had been abducted and then barely managed to get away with his life.

We still didn't have the jump drive, and I still didn't know what was on it. But I was exceedingly grateful that Grayson was okay.

Thirty minutes later, Velma still hadn't made it into the office, nor was she answering her phone.

I knew when Oscar walked into our office that he was worried.

"I need the two of you to go check out Velma's apartment. I'm going to call a couple of her friends and see if they know where she is."

I rose from my desk and nodded. I'd feel better if we went and checked things out also.

Michael didn't say anything as he walked beside me. Before we slipped out the office door, Oscar handed us something.

"This is a key to Velma's apartment." Warning stained Oscar's voice. "She gave me a copy, just so someone would have a backup. Use it if you have to."

Velma and Oscar were closer than I had suspected. I knew the two had a past connection and that Oscar had helped her out of an abusive relationship. But I had no idea that the two were practically family.

I slid the key into my pocket, and Michael and I stepped outside.

As we did, I prayed that the bad feeling brewing in my gut was simply an overreaction.

———

VELMA'S APARTMENT was an older complex known as Anchors Reach. It was located on the river, three stories high, and each unit had a private balcony on the back side and an outside entrance at the front.

"Have you been here before?" I asked Michael as we climbed from his minivan and started toward the building.

"I haven't." Michael glanced around. "Nice location, though. I'm thinking I need a pay raise. Oscar's been holding back on us."

"Me too." Although, prior to this, I had thought I was getting paid pretty well.

Perspective.

On the other hand, maybe this was what being frugal could lead to. Since Velma didn't spend money on food, toilet paper, or clothing, I suppose she could pour her entire paycheck into living here.

That didn't quite seem to fit the image of Velma that I knew, however.

"I wish I didn't feel so nervous," I told Michael as we climbed the stairs to the second floor.

"Maybe Velma's not feeling well and her phone died," Michael suggested.

I wondered if he really believed that. Michael wasn't the naïve type. His street smarts seemed to be ingrained in him like the tattoos across his arms.

He rang the bell, and we waited.

No one answered.

He rang the bell again, and we waited some more.

Again, no answer.

This time, Michael raised his hand to knock at the door while yelling, "Velma? It's Michael and Elliot. We're here to check on you."

When there was still no answer, I handed the key to Michael and he slid the key into the lock.

Slowly, he pushed the door open.

The good news was that the place looked neat, and there were no signs that anybody had been violent inside.

That only made me feel better for a moment, though. Because I knew that something was wrong.

Michael stepped inside. "Velma? Are you here?"

Still no answer.

We crept inside even farther. I stayed behind Michael, just to be on the safe side.

As we walked through her living room, I glanced around. For someone who was a cheapskate, Velma had found some great deals on the furniture. Though nothing matched, the coral couch had cheerful pillows. It appeared she'd painted a coffee table and bookshelves a pleasant white, and she'd added throws over two other chairs to make them blend in better.

Maybe I should have given Velma more credit when it came to her money-saving ways. In fact, maybe I could learn from her.

"Velma?" Michael called again.

Still no response.

Every step I took deeper into the apartment caused my muscles to tighten even more.

Michael pushed open the door to the bathroom. Empty. He pushed open the door to the first bedroom. Also empty. He pushed open the door to the last bedroom. It was also empty.

Unless Velma was hiding under a bed or inside a closet, she wasn't here.

And the very bad feeling in my gut only grew larger.

CHAPTER TWO

"SHOULD WE CALL THE POLICE?" I turned toward Michael as we stood in Velma's living room.

Michael glanced around the space once more before sighing. "Let's give Oscar a few more minutes to see if he touched base with her friends. In the meantime, I want to check out the kitchen again."

I wasn't sure what he was getting at since Velma clearly hadn't been in the kitchen when we passed.

Despite that, I followed Michael and waited for further instructions.

"Check the trashcan," he told me. "See how fresh anything in there looks. Wear gloves. If something did happen to Velma, we don't want to mess up any evidence."

I'd actually brought some disposable gloves with me this time. I slipped them on and used my foot to push the release lever to lift the trashcan top. It popped open, and I peered inside.

I was hoping to see something that screamed some type of answer. Instead, I saw some coffee grounds and a discarded container of vanilla ice cream.

"Anything?" Michael peered over the fridge door.

"Coffee grounds?"

"Touch them. See if they're warm."

I didn't ask any questions, just did as he asked. "They're cold. There's an old container of ice cream."

"Open it. See if it's moldy yet."

Again, I did as he told me. "No mold."

He closed the refrigerator and walked toward the sink. A coffee cup sat in the rack beside it, but nothing else.

Michael frowned and turned, crossing his arms over his chest as his gaze scanned the rest of the room.

"What are you thinking?" I tried to read his body language but couldn't.

"If the coffee grounds had been warm, that might have meant Velma was here this morning. I checked the coffee pot. It's cold also. The ice cream container wasn't moldy yet, so it's not that old. It doesn't look like Velma was here today, if I had to guess."

It sounded like good deductive reasoning to me.

"Could she have stayed with somebody last night?" I didn't know Velma well enough to know if she had some type of secret boyfriend or not. But it seemed like a possibility we should explore.

"Velma isn't the type to spend the night with anybody," Michael said. "And she doesn't have a boyfriend—unless he's a total secret. But Velma's never been that great at keeping those kinds of secrets."

His words rang with truth. "So what do we do now?"

Michael pulled out his phone, his gaze fixed with decisiveness. "I'm going to call Oscar."

I stepped closer so I could hear the conversation. I desperately hoped this was all a misunderstanding— even though I knew it wasn't.

Michael put the phone on speaker.

"Anything?" Michael asked Oscar.

"Nobody has seen Velma since last night," Oscar said. "She went to dinner at a friend's house. Her friend— Cindy is her name—said that she left her place at ten thirty to go home. No one has seen or heard from her since then. It's like she *vanished*." He said vanished with an accent, as if it were a foreign word when it wasn't.

"She's not here at her apartment," Michael said. "It doesn't look like she was here this morning."

"Walk through the parking lot. See if her car is there," Oscar said. "I'll stay on the phone while you do."

Michael and I stepped outside. From the second-floor

walkway, I scanned the lot. On the third row back, I spotted the dark sedan Velma drove.

I pointed it out to Michael. "Her car is still here."

His jaw hardened as he relayed the information to Oscar.

"I'm going to call the police," Oscar said. "It won't take them long to get to Velma's place. Before they get there, look at anything else you need to look at in the apartment and look at her car. Understand?"

The serious tone of Oscar's voice made my spine straighten. He was worried about Velma and thought something had happened to her.

Part of me wanted to remain in denial. I wanted to pretend that she was okay. That this was just a misunderstanding.

But I knew that would be naïve. I knew the implications of what was going on here, whether or not I wanted to acknowledge them out loud.

Velma was in trouble. If I denied it, I'd be in a bubble. I prayed she was fine, and that life would be kind, but I knew this was no time to be blind.

Oh, no. I was rhyming.

It was what I always did when I felt stressed and anxious. My father had taught me the technique as a means of distracting myself from otherwise overwhelming thoughts.

But no amount of rhyming was going to make this any better.

"ANYTHING IN THE BACKSEAT?"

I stood, pulling myself from the back of Velma's car. Michael had managed to pick the lock so we could search the inside.

But it appeared it was all for nothing. "It's clean, and there's no evidence that anything happened," I told him.

Michael climbed out of the front seat, straightened, and let out a sigh. The sunlight hit his face, causing him to squint. He pulled his backward baseball cap off and turned it so the bill covered his eyes.

I knew what his body language meant. He hadn't found anything either.

"She left her friend's place at ten thirty last night." Michael stared into the distance as if his thoughts had enveloped him. "Based on her car, it appears Velma made it back here last night. So what happened to her between the time Velma returned and this morning?"

The answer to that question was on the tip of my tongue, but I dared not say the words "Beltway Killer" out loud. Instead, I asked, "Do we need to look at anything else inside her apartment? Before the police get here?"

"I think we've looked at all we can. If Velma's gone . . ." Michael's voice trailed like he didn't want to finish his sentence either.

But I knew what he was going to say.

He was thinking what I was thinking—that if Velma was gone, her disappearance could be connected to the Beltway Killer.

I thought we were in the clear. I thought that because nobody from the softball team had disappeared, that the rose and knot Michael and I had found had all been a misunderstanding or a bad joke.

But I might be wrong.

The killer could have had another target in his sights this whole time. I'd just never imagined that it might be Velma.

A sick feeling gurgled in my stomach at the thought of it.

Before Michael and I could consider more of our options, Oscar pulled up in his BMW. Immediately following him were two patrol cars.

He nodded at us before walking with the officers up to Velma's place. As he did, another car pulled into the lot, an unmarked police car. I only knew because Detective Dylan Hunter was driving it.

The tension in me pulled tighter.

Hunter and I had been getting to know each other.

Taking it slow. Unsure if either of us were ready for a relationship.

But then somehow Michael and I had happened. I hadn't figured out the best way to tell Hunter that information yet.

Which made seeing him again right now feel a little bit awkward.

As he climbed from his car, he glanced over at Michael and me. Something changed in his gaze. His eyes widened, and I suspected Hunter knew something was going on between Michael and me, even though I hadn't said a word.

Michael and I paced toward the stairway, knowing we'd cross paths with Hunter there. Sure enough, we did.

A knot formed in my chest as I came face-to-face with the man. He wore his typical black slacks and blue button-up shirt with the sleeves rolled to his elbows. I'd always thought the man had a Chris Evans vibe with his classic good looks and reserved manner.

"Elliot." Hunter slowed his steps when he saw us. "Michael."

"Good morning." I tried to force a smile, but it wouldn't come.

He didn't tell us to stop when we followed him on his walk toward Velma's apartment. But his formal tone when he said hello set me on edge. I couldn't worry about that right now.

"I heard that a colleague of yours is missing," Hunter called over his shoulder.

"She hasn't been seen since ten thirty last night, best we know," Michael said.

"I'm going to check out her apartment, but I'll need to talk to both of you later and get your statements." Hunter gave us a pointed look, no doubt used to Michael and me interrupting his investigations.

"Of course," I muttered.

His gaze remained on me a moment longer before he paused several feet from Velma's door. "I need to ask you two to stay here."

"No problem," I insisted, not telling him we'd already been inside. That would come up soon enough.

As he walked away, Michael turned to me. "Did you tell him about us?"

"Not yet." I leaned against the wooden railing behind me.

Michael locked his gaze with mine. "Are you going to?"

"Seems like I should. But it also feels awkward since Hunter and I weren't really dating, just talking."

Michael tilted his head, a pinched expression on his face. "You should probably still say something to him. Guys can be clueless sometimes. True fact."

"You're probably right. But now's not the time. I'll try to do that a little bit later."

Right now, I glanced at Velma's door and waited. I wanted to hear what Oscar thought. What the police thought. What Hunter thought.

I only prayed that their conclusions were more optimistic than mine.

CHAPTER THREE

TWENTY MINUTES LATER, Hunter emerged from Velma's apartment. Though Michael and I waited near the stairway, Oscar had lingered just outside the door.

He and Hunter exchanged a few words before Hunter paced away, his phone to his ear.

I was dying to know if the police had found anything that Michael and I hadn't.

Until I could talk to Oscar, I'd have to wait on hearing that answer. But with every second that passed, I knew the chances of finding Velma alive decreased steadily.

And that wasn't okay.

Michael leaned closer to me and whispered, "You hanging in?"

I nodded, even though I didn't know if it was the truth. I almost felt like everything had both gone still around me and was spinning like crazy as well. I knew it didn't make sense, but I couldn't shake that feeling that my world was tilting on its axis.

If Velma had been abducted—and I felt certain she had been—then we needed a plan on how to find her. I didn't even know exactly where to start, but I hoped Michael and Oscar might have some good ideas. Doing nothing wasn't an option here.

Hunter breezed past Michael and me, his phone still pressed to his ear. As he did, Oscar approached us.

"Ordinarily, it would be too soon to launch a missing person investigation," Oscar started. "But, because of everything going on in the area with the Beltway Killer, the police are going to start looking into Velma's disappearance now."

"How can we help?" I rushed.

Oscar motioned for me to keep my voice down. "The police don't want us to help. But, of course, we're going to. I thought maybe we could meet back at the office and figure out our next plan of action."

"Did Hunter say anything else we should know about?" I couldn't stand the thought of waiting until we were back at the office to learn potentially pertinent information.

"Not really. But we're going to need to talk to Velma's neighbors." Oscar glanced at the cops lingering in the distance and frowned. "We're not going to have a chance to do that—not now. We'll come back later."

I stared at the parking lot, trying to picture what might have played out. "We have to assume that Velma was able to get back here since her car was in the lot. So, the most likely scenario, is that she got out of her car, and, in between the car and her apartment, something happened."

Oscar frowned. "You're probably right. But we can't leave any stone unturned."

"What are these stones you're talking about?" I asked, absolutely confused.

Michael leaned closer, the hint of a smile playing on his lips. "Oscar just means he wants to make sure we scrutinize everything and make sure not to miss any details."

I suppose that made sense.

Just then, Hunter appeared again, shoving his phone back in his pocket. He pulled out a small notebook as he approached us.

"Elliot," he started. "Michael. I'm going to need to get a statement from both of you. Separately, please."

I nodded, knowing this was part of the deal.

But what I really wanted to do was to start looking for Velma right now.

I SAT with Hunter in his car and recounted everything that had happened. As I did, he took notes and nodded and offered noncommittal responses. It was strange because it almost seemed like we weren't even friends. That we hadn't hung out together.

Everything felt stiff and professional. But maybe that was the way it should be. This was a serious investigation into a potentially dangerous crime. Personal relationships had no role here.

When I finished, Hunter clicked his pen, closed his notebook, and turned toward me with those serious eyes of his. "Thank you, Elliot."

I stared at him, not ready to finish this conversation yet. I still felt like there were things that needed to be said. "Do you think it's the Beltway Killer?"

"Too early to say." He shrugged noncommittally.

I couldn't let him off that easily. "But that rose with the rope around it . . . it was found at the baseball field. This guy could have known that Driscoll and Associates was investigating. The flower could have been left as a sign that Velma was going to be the next victim."

It seemed pretty clear to me. I needed to light a fire on this investigation.

"Believe me, we're going to take all of that into consideration." Hunter's voice sounded reassuring. "The best thing that you can do right now is just to lie low."

"You know that we're not going to be able to do that.

Velma is our friend, our coworker. How long do we have before he . . . ?" I couldn't finish the question.

"If this is the Beltway Killer, he usually keeps his victims alive a couple weeks."

"So we have approximately fourteen days before Velma dies, and even longer than that before her body will be discovered." A sick feeling gurgled in my stomach. It sounded surreal to say those words.

Hunter's grim look told me everything that I needed to know.

I swallowed, though my throat felt swollen and unco-operative. "Are you going to tell the media?"

"That's not my call," Hunter said. "I need to go back to my captain and talk to him about everything. He'll make the decision."

I shook my head, and my hand went to my forehead. I rubbed it, trying to soothe away the tension headache that had formed. "I can't believe this is happening."

Hunter's hand covered my shoulder. "I know. And I'm sorry, Elliot."

My head popped up as I remembered his connection with this killer. The man had murdered Hunter's fiancée. How could I not have thought about that earlier?

"How are you doing, Hunter?" I studied his face, honestly wanting to know. I couldn't help but think he was carrying all his burdens alone.

He looked away, his lips pressed together and his gaze

burdened. "I'm trying to separate personal and professional. The captain will probably take me off this case. But, of course, I'm trying to find answers. I never stopped trying to find answers."

"Of course."

"The FBI will probably be brought in on this," he continued. "I expect our department will be removed from lead on this case and only be used as support."

"I'm so sorry that you're going through this." I touched his hand, knowing that this had to be so hard on him. I hated to think about how much he was suffering.

"Thanks." Despite the sincerity in his tone, the word still sounded tight and clipped.

If he opened up too much, everything might pour out. I knew what that was like. But I couldn't push him.

My thoughts shifted. I remembered my developing relationship with Michael, and I wondered if Hunter and I needed to talk about that.

Maybe.

But I also knew this would be a horrible time to bring that up. There were other more important things going on.

Hunter released a long breath and glanced back at me, something seeming to mentally shift inside him. "I need to keep investigating. But I'll call you if I have any more questions. And, in the meantime, stay out of trouble, okay?"

"Of course." I said the words easily, as if someone had simply reminded me to take my trash out.

"I mean it, Elliot. Stay safe, okay?" His gaze locked onto mine.

"And I mean it when I tell you that I will. Or that I will do my best, at least." I offered a feeble shrug.

Hunter offered one final "goodbye" before I climbed out.

I really hoped that when he said stay out of trouble, he didn't mean that I should stay out of this investigation. Because there was absolutely no way I was going to be able to do that.

Not while knowing Velma was involved.

CHAPTER FOUR

OSCAR, Michael, and I met back at the office fifteen minutes later. I'd never seen Oscar look as intense as he did as he stared at Michael and me from behind his massive throne—I mean, desk. His nostrils flared, his forehead furrowed, and his lips pressed tight.

"We're not going to be able to do anything at her complex right now," Oscar started, tapping a pudgy finger on his desk. "Police are crawling all over it. So we're going to need to figure out something else."

"What do you want us to do?" Michael asked.

"Great question. For starters, I'd like the two of you to see if you can find any security camera footage around her apartment."

For the first time since I'd known Oscar, he almost seemed like a leader, like someone who was in charge of more than just financing our operations or acting as a figurehead. As Michael would say, the man had finally stepped up to the plate.

"It would have been dark outside," Michael said. "I'm not sure if we're going to be able to tell anything from any of that security footage. But it's still worth a shot."

Oscar tapped his finger against the desk again. "I already talked to several of her friends. None of them have heard from her. We don't have the capabilities to trace her cell phone, though I'm sure that's one of the first things the police will try to do."

A moment of silence fell between us all.

"I think we all know who is responsible for this." I hesitated to say the words out loud, but we couldn't keep dancing around the fire like we didn't have a guinea pig to roast. "This has to be the work of the Beltway Killer."

Oscar visibly flinched at my harsh words. "You might be right. But I don't want to think like that."

"It's the only thing that makes sense," I continued. "I really doubt we're going to make much headway by talking to her friends or looking at this security footage. I think the best way we dive into this case is by examining the Beltway Killer and all his previous victims. Certainly, there are things about each victim that tie those cases together. We need to look at the locations where the victims were left. Look at timelines. Do everything we can to pinpoint who this guy is."

"Elliot," Michael started, a slight hesitation to his voice as he leaned toward me. "I love your enthusiasm, but the police haven't been able to find this guy for the past three years. Why do you think that we are going to be able to?"

"Because we're Driscoll and Associates." My voice rose with conviction. "That's what we do. We close cases. We don't give up. And, now, one of our own has been taken. It's more important than ever."

Oscar's eyebrows shot up after I finished my speech, and both men offered a slow, surprised nod.

"You're right." Oscar continued to slowly nod. "That's probably going to be our best plan of action right now. We need to start examining this guy. Maybe we can even talk to the families of some of these victims and try to find some commonalities among them."

I stood, happy that we finally had a feasible plan and eager to get going on it. "I can start putting together a dossier of those people. Then maybe Michael and I can visit the first victim's family and continue down the list."

Oscar nodded. "I like that. While you do that, I'm going to call Velma's friend Cindy again and confirm the details about last night. Then I'm going to call Kitty Kight."

"Why would you call Kitty Kight?" The reporter had done an article on the charity softball game that Michael and I had participated in this past weekend.

"She did a story on the Beltway Killer. Maybe she can also offer us some insights."

"It sounds like it's worth a shot," I said.

"And as you guys do that, I'll call the rest of Velma's friends and see if they have any information," Michael said. "Maybe she said something last night that might give us a clue."

With that said, we all stood and went to our respective work areas.

We had no time to waste on getting to work on this.

MICHAEL and I decided to go back to the beginning of the Beltway Killer's murder spree—back to victim number one.

Three years had passed, and five women were now dead.

He only struck areas around the Capital Beltway, and his last victim had been found in Storm River just a week ago.

Michael and I headed out to talk to the family of Trisha Thomas, his first victim. Trisha had been twenty-four years old, black, and she had a fabulous smile. From everything I'd read about her online, she'd been vivacious and had the whole world ahead of her.

The killer seemed to target women who were relatively alone. That wasn't to say his victims didn't have families, but those units weren't necessarily close by. These were women who were on their own, who were attractive, and who were in their twenties.

After Trisha had been killed, her mom and brother had moved to the area from South Carolina in hopes of finding the real killer. I'd set up the appointment with them, explaining that we were private investigators looking into the Beltway Killer. I'd been careful not to mention that somebody else was missing. That wasn't my news to share.

But I still couldn't stop thinking about the fact that Velma was missing.

I frowned as I stared out the window at the road as it blurred by. Velma was a character within herself. Her antics made me laugh, and I'd always liked the woman, even though we were just starting to get to know each other.

She had curly blonde hair that she liked to wear piled on top of her head, she liked flashy clothes and big earrings, and she spoke with a Southern drawl.

When I closed my eyes, I sometimes started to imagine where she was right now. Or what was happening to her. Or how scared she must be.

Did she know the person who had taken her? Did she realize what was coming?

Nausea roiled in me at the thought of it.

"I know this is hard." Michael rested his hand on my knee.

As soon as I felt his touch, my muscles turned to gelatin. He had that effect on me, and our relationship was still new enough that I reveled in the flutters in my stomach. I reached down and laced my fingers through his.

The action was still novel and didn't quite feel normal. Yet, on the other hand, it seemed so natural.

I'd thought of Michael as a great friend for so long. I hadn't realized that, beneath the surface, there might have been something more.

He was the one bright spot in what otherwise felt like a tumultuous time of change in my life.

Had it only been a few hours ago that I'd thought this day would be promising?

Who would have guessed I'd be so, so wrong?

"I just can't stop thinking about Velma . . ." I murmured.

"I know. Me too."

"I feel like there's this ticking time bomb in my lap, like I need to find her or it's going to be horrible."

"We have to stay positive."

"But it's like you said earlier," I continued, still not done sorting out my thoughts. "If the police haven't been able to track down this guy, what makes us think that we can?"

As we pulled to a stop, Michael brushed a hair out of my eyes, looping it behind my ear. "You've got great intuition, Elliot. Use it on this case. Use those powers of observation that you have. Maybe you'll see something the police didn't see. That's what makes me think we can. We're a good team."

"I hope so."

But that thought also made an unseen pressure push on me. I'd just begun to experience the feeling, and I already felt like it might break me.

But I wasn't going to let it do that.

I was stronger than that feeling. I was going to push through this.

And one way or another, I was going to find Velma.

CHAPTER FIVE

TRISHA THOMAS'S mother and brother lived in an older apartment complex about fifteen minutes from downtown DC, in the Georgetown area. The place was well-kept, and the cheerful wreath on the door with the sprigs of honeysuckle around it seemed to indicate hope had begun to grow again in their lives, even after this tragedy.

Trisha's mom, Regina, met us at the door with a dull look in her gaze. The woman was probably in her fifties. Her salt-and-pepper-colored hair was pulled back into a tight bun, and her thin features looked drawn.

She led us inside, seated us on a navy blue couch, and brought us iced tea. Her son, Peter, emerged from a back bedroom a few minutes later, an equally grim expression on his equally thin face.

After a few minutes of chitchat, it was time to talk about the real reason Michael and I had come.

"I know this is a difficult conversation, but would you mind telling us about your daughter?" Michael started.

"No, not at all," Regina said. "We want to keep her memory alive and so many people want to skirt around any conversations about her. I'd rather cry than forget."

"Makes perfect sense," I murmured.

"Peter and I moved here when Trisha disappeared." Regina ran a tissue beneath her eyes as she began. "We wanted to do whatever we could to find her. We just never thought that it would turn out like this."

My heart pounded with compassion. I could only begin to imagine what this family had been through. Their ordeal was the stuff of nightmares. Unfortunately, I understood parts of their grief a little too well.

"What was Trisha doing here?" I asked before taking a sip of my drink. As I did, the flavor of peaches swirled over my taste buds, reminding me of summer and carefree days and . . . home.

I immediately liked Regina.

"Trisha had just graduated from college with a degree in French," Regina continued. "I always asked her what she planned on doing with that degree, and she had no idea. But I couldn't change her mind, and I wasn't paying for college so she could do what she wanted."

"Was she working?" Michael's voice sounded low and soft as he asked the question.

For a tough guy, his compassion always amazed me.

"It wasn't a surprise to anyone when she wasn't able to find a job in her field. She took a position as a receptionist at an auto dealership until she could find something else. But she really liked this area. That's why she decided to stay after graduation from Howard University."

"Did she have a lot of friends here?" I tried to put together a mental picture of what Trisha was like.

"She wasn't the type to hang out with just anybody. But she probably had three or four friends that she considered close. When she wasn't working, they were like family to her." Peter paused and shifted. "At least, they had been up until a few weeks before she passed."

That was an interesting comment. "What do you mean?"

"I guess Trisha and one of her friends had some type of falling out over a guy," her brother said. "You know how it is when you're friends with someone of the opposite sex. One person wants it to be platonic and the other doesn't, and then things get all messed up."

Hearing him say the words caused a rush of heat across my skin. I didn't want whatever was happening between Michael and I now to mess up our friendship. I prayed that wouldn't be the case.

"One of the guys—his name was John—liked Trisha, but Trisha's friend Natalie liked John. I really think that their friendships would have returned to normal eventually." Peter's voice cracked. "They just never had a chance to fix things."

"Did anything strange happen to Trisha in the days leading up to her death?" Michael asked. "I know you've been over all these things with the police, and I also know that you weren't living here at the time. But did you hear anything that might give us a clearer picture?"

"I wish I could give you something." Regina frowned and played with a crocheted pillow she held in her lap. "We did talk every day. But she never mentioned being afraid or that she'd met anybody new or anything that raised any suspicions. It was like she was living her normal life, and one day she just disappeared."

She pressed the tissue into her eyes again as more moisture streamed there.

Her words reminded me an awful lot of Velma, though.

"I'm so sorry for your loss." I knew my words were inadequate. There was nothing I could say in a situation like this that would make her feel better. But I could try to catch the person responsible for her daughter's death.

"If you think of anything else," Michael said, "please give us a call."

Regina's eyes drew up to meet ours. "Someone else is missing, isn't she?"

Michael and I exchanged glances. I wasn't sure how much we could say, how much the police wanted us to say. I didn't want to put the investigation in jeopardy.

"I do believe there's been another development in the case," Michael finally admitted.

Regina stood, a fire igniting in her gaze. "Tell me. Was someone else taken?"

As tension built in me, I waited for Michael to take the lead. I wasn't sure what the correct protocol was in this situation.

Michael frowned. "We think so, but it's not official yet. The woman who was taken . . . she was our friend."

"God bless you both as you look for her." Regina's shoulders slumped, and more tears leaked from her eyes. "I hope you find her. I really do. Because if you don't . . . your lives will never be the same again."

AN HOUR LATER, Oscar met us at an upscale seafood restaurant called The Quarterdeck so we could discuss what we'd learned. The place was decorated with a nautical theme and all wood surroundings—from the floor to the walls to the ceiling.

Oscar didn't ask Michael or I what we wanted to eat.

Instead, he'd ordered a variety of dishes and appetizers we could share.

The truth was, I figured none of us felt like eating, though the scent of fried seafood was a little too appetizing right now.

Our first priority was to compare notes and see if there was anything that might help us find Velma.

Oscar had gone to talk to the family of the second victim, and I hoped he'd learned more than we had.

"So, the second victim's name was Gloria Wilson," Oscar started, dunking a jumbo shrimp into some cocktail sauce.

I pictured the woman in my head. She had red hair the color of fire and green eyes like clovers. She'd been a waitress at a dive bar outside of DC.

"Her father lives down in Richmond," Oscar continued. "I was able to talk to him for a few minutes. I wish he'd had something to share that would help us, but there was very little he knew. He hadn't spoken with his daughter for almost a year when she disappeared."

"She was like the rest of them?" I asked. "A loner with no one really to look out for her . . ."

Oscar nodded solemnly before nearly mauling the shrimp. "That's right."

My heart seemed to lodge in my throat. I picked up a crusty piece of bread, but I wasn't sure I'd be able to scoop any crab dip onto it. "I never thought of Velma that way. She had us."

The frown on Oscar's face grew deeper. "She did. But that was only at work. After hours . . . she did her own thing. Just like we all do."

The lump in my throat grew larger at his ominous words.

Did Oscar know—or suspect—that Michael and I were dating? I felt certain he would fire us if he did. I knew all about the hazards of a workplace romance. Yet here I was, unable to walk away from this thing that was developing between Michael and me.

I doubted that was Oscar's biggest concern at the moment.

I cleared my throat. "Still, I just hate to think of Velma that way."

"We all do." Oscar picked up another shrimp. "That's why we have to find her. We're all she's got."

"What do we do now?" Michael leaned back in his seat, his arm casually draped around the back of my wooden chair. He'd eaten a mini crab cake already but didn't seem interested in any other food. "There are three other families we could talk to."

"True," Oscar said.

Michael glanced at me. "You've already talked to Hunter about his fiancée, haven't you?"

That familiar heat rose from my neck all the way to

my cheeks. "I have. He doesn't like to talk about what happened to her, and I'm sure he doesn't want us investigating. I'm not really sure what good it would do if we tried to talk to him about her anymore."

"You're probably right." Oscar nodded slowly, stabbing the last crab cake with his fork. "The only other thing I can think of is that we need to go back to Velma's apartment complex. The police are probably gone by now, and we need to talk to everybody who lives there. Maybe somebody saw something."

I hoped so.

"And by the way." Oscar nodded at Michael. "No arms around the backs of chairs. Don't you know how prevalent sexual harassment cases are?"

As Michael removed his arm, the lump in my throat grew larger.

CHAPTER SIX

IT WAS a truth universally known that people were more inclined to talk to ordinary citizens than they were official police detectives. That was the only thing that gave me hope as we approached Velma's apartment complex after our late lunch.

To my shock, Oscar had joined Michael and me. He'd insisted that we should go door to door to find answers and that three people worked faster than two.

Two police cars were still on the scene, but I wasn't sure exactly why. There didn't appear to be any evidence here, at least from what I'd seen earlier.

I hoped that the officers didn't try to stop us.

I had ridden over with Michael. As we climbed from his minivan, I took a moment to look around.

There had to be at least a hundred apartments at this

complex. It would take a while to knock on every door. Plus, most likely everybody wouldn't be home. The task almost seemed overwhelming as I thought about it.

But Velma was worth it.

"We should split up," Oscar said as he joined us near Michael's minivan. "That way we can save time."

"Why don't we each take one floor?" I suggested. "We should make a note on our phones of which residents don't answer so we can come back later and talk to them. I'm assuming a lot of people aren't home right now, and those could be the very people who saw something. The fact is, some residents may not have even realized they saw something."

Oscar's eyebrows flickered up, almost as if he was impressed with my assumption.

"Let's do it. I'll take the first floor." Oscar nodded as he started that way.

As Michael and I headed to the stairway, he said, "If at any point you feel like you're in danger, yell, and I'll be right there."

My heart warmed at the concern in his words. "Thanks. I appreciate you looking out for me."

He winked. "Always."

His words made me suck in a quick breath. Hearing the affection in his voice made me want to pinch myself. Michael had been in front of me this whole time, and I hadn't seen him as a romantic interest.

Yet I couldn't imagine anyone more perfect for me.

When Oscar faded from sight and we'd cleared the first stairway, Michael tugged me behind the edge of the stairway and leaned close.

Almost like he wanted to kiss me.

But he didn't.

He only teased me.

When he stepped back, my heart fluttered from his nearness.

"You're so bad." I jabbed a finger in his chest.

"I just hate that we're keeping this a secret. Keeping *us* a secret."

"It's for the best," I reminded him. New relationships were too fragile. We needed to be on solid ground before we announced ourselves to others who would be affected —like Chloe or Oscar.

He nodded, that tender look still present in his eyes. "You're right. We should get to work. But really—be careful."

We said that to each other almost as much as most normal people said hello, goodbye, and thank you.

As he left me on the second floor, I stared at the row of doors in front of me. I had to get busy. There was no time to waste here, and we had a huge task in front of us.

I prayed we would find some answers . . . because it didn't seem like we had that many options right now. Velma's life depended on us being at our best.

I couldn't bear the thought of letting her down.

TWO HOURS LATER, the three of us had hit every door at the complex.

No one had seen anything.

Only a couple people even knew who Velma was and had met her. Several people looked interested and concerned but knew nothing. One seemed hungry for gossip and kept asking questions.

But as Oscar, Michael, and I stood in the parking lot, I felt the defeat hanging around us.

This wasn't the outcome any of us wanted. The outcome of no progress. No forward movement. No direction.

I crossed my arms and leaned against Oscar's BMW, not ready to give up yet. "There has to be something else we can do. I just can't go home now and sleep like nothing happened."

"Me neither." Michael hovered beside me, looking equally as concerned.

Oscar let out a long breath, sweat sprinkled across his wide forehead. This was the most work he'd done in a long time, and it was good to see him sweat.

"We can keep talking to people but, without any other clues, I'm at a loss as to what else we might be able to do."

I hated to admit it, but so was I. The timeline might help us in the long run, but it wouldn't help us to find Velma now. And that was what we needed to do.

The only thing that comforted me was knowing that the killer didn't usually kill his victims right away. He kept them alive, for some reason.

I shuddered to think what that might mean. But, if I understood correctly, most of the victims hadn't been mutilated. I supposed that was good news.

"How about this?" Oscar straightened. "We go our separate ways now. We can each brainstorm on our own tonight. When we come together tomorrow morning, maybe we'll have some more ideas."

Michael and I both stared at him. I'd wanted more leadership. More guidance.

But that wasn't what we'd gotten.

Oscar shrugged, as if sensing our disappointment. "That's all I know to do right now. With no clues . . . our hands are tied."

I hated to admit it, but Oscar was right. There really wasn't anything else we could do right now. We needed something to give us direction before we took the next step. No one had seen anything. No evidence had been left. There were no leads we could follow. This wasn't acceptable.

"On the way home, I'll swing by and talk to a friend of the fourth victim," Oscar said. "The other victim . . . the one that was just found last week . . . I'm not sure her family is going to be willing to talk yet. Her death is too fresh."

"Besides, from what I read, her family is down in Texas," I added. "According to what I heard, she had no friends here."

"Which again makes this more complicated," Oscar said. "Still, she had some coworkers. She had neighbors. We should talk to anyone we can."

Michael and I both nodded.

A few minutes later, after Oscar drove away, Michael and I turned to each other. We didn't have to say a word to know what the other was thinking.

This is our worst-case scenario. Our friend had been taken, and we were powerless to help her.

"I have to go pick up Chloe in a minute." Michael stepped toward me and rubbed my arms. After glancing over his shoulder and checking to see if Oscar was out of sight, he pulled me into a hug. "Are you holding up okay?"

"I guess."

"Storms eventually pass," Michael murmured. "It never feels like it when you're in the middle of them, though."

I knew he told the truth. I was definitely at the point where I felt as if the storm stretched on for miles and miles. Swirling yet remaining stationary—just like the overwhelming feeling I'd experienced earlier.

Michael stepped back and studied my face. "How about we get pizza and take it back to my house and hang out? We can talk there for a little while and see if we can come up with something. I know Chloe would love to see you."

I smiled at the sound of Chloe's name. "That sounds nice. But drop me off at the office first so I can get my car. That way I don't have to worry about getting home."

"It's a plan." Michael gently pressed a kiss to my forehead before backing away. "Let's go."

CHAPTER SEVEN

"HENRY KEEPS PULLING MY PONYTAIL." Chloe put another piece of pizza on her plate and rolled her eyes. "He drives me crazy."

I felt a smile tugging at my lips. I loved hearing Chloe's perspective on life. She was always so full of energy and love. What was there not to love about this little girl?

"I know it sounds strange." Michael leaned toward her from across the kitchen table, as if sharing a secret. "But sometimes when boys do things like that, it's actually because they like you."

Chloe twisted her lips and narrowed her eyes. "That makes no sense."

"I know," Michael said. "Life is really confusing sometimes, isn't it?"

She lifted her slice of pizza, about to take another bite. Before she did, she chirped, "Yes, it is. Do you ever pull Elliot's ponytail, Daddy?"

He let out a quick laugh. "No, I like doing much more annoying things to her like staring at her until she blushes."

I elbowed him.

Chloe shrugged, unaffected. "I'm really glad I'm having pizza right now. Especially with the two of you."

Michael and I exchanged a smile. Michael hadn't told Chloe yet that we were dating. We were going to get to know each other just a little better before we broke the news to her. The last thing I wanted was for Chloe to get too attached and then for something to happen between Michael and me.

I understood that protecting his daughter was one of the most noble things Michael could do.

"Did you guys have a good day?" Chloe looked back and forth between the two of us with an almost comical look on her face. I was convinced she was a mini adult.

I wanted to tell the girl that things were great. But I remembered Velma, and I knew I couldn't do that. There was too much at stake right now.

"It was another one of those days where we had to work really hard." Michael's voice turned serious. "But that's what you do when you believe in something, right? You work hard."

Chloe offered another little eye roll. "You always say that, Daddy."

"Only because it's true."

Before we could talk anymore, the doorbell rang. Michael excused himself to answer. I couldn't help but wonder who might be here. His parents maybe?

I hadn't met them yet. Truthfully, I was a little nervous about being introduced. They were the pastors at a mega church in the area, and, from everything I'd seen and heard about them, they were the picture of the perfect Christian power couple.

The problem was that I'd been around long enough to know there was no such thing as the perfect Christian family or couple. Something about seeing people try so hard to fit that image turned my stomach.

When Michael didn't return after a few minutes, I decided to check on him. Had Oscar stopped by? What if something was wrong?

I excused myself from Chloe and peered around the corner.

I spotted Michael standing in the doorway. A woman stood in front of him. At least, she did for a second. The next instant, her arms flew around Michael.

I heard him mutter, "Roxy . . ."

I sucked in a breath. That was when I knew who she was.

Chloe's mom.

The woman who had disappeared almost seven years ago and hadn't been heard from since then.

What was she doing here now?

I TRIED NOT TO PANIC. But I didn't know what to do. In fact, I wanted to disappear.

But that wasn't an option right now.

The love of his life has returned. The one who left Michael scorned and burned. Are there lessons there that still need to be learned? Should I be concerned?

"Who is it?" Chloe appeared beside me.

My heart pounded harder as I motioned for her to keep her voice down. Did Michael want Chloe to see Roxy? I had no idea, which left me speechless for a moment.

With one last glance at the door, I put my arm around the girl's shoulders and led her back into the kitchen. "It looks like an old friend of your dad's is here. Why don't we keep eating our pizza while they talk?"

Chloe shrugged and went back to the table to finish eating.

I mentally released the breath I'd been holding. That had been close. I'd bought a little bit of time, at least.

"She was pretty." Chloe picked a pepperoni from the top of her pizza slice.

Even she'd seen enough to notice that.

Chloe told the truth. Roxy was a knockout, as people said. I hadn't any doubt that would be the case, however.

I figured that Chloe got her looks from her mom: the long blonde hair, the bright smile, and the pretty blue eyes.

Michael was handsome too. But he was thick with defined muscles and a squarish jaw that was framed with dark hair.

Chloe looked nothing like him.

I tried to focus on Chloe and what she was saying to me, something about how she wanted to get a dog, but all I could think about was Michael and Roxy. Why in the world had the woman appeared again after all these years? What sense did it make?

I didn't know. Nor did I have any clue if this would change things between Michael and me.

Yes, I was going there. Maybe the leap seemed too big, but I knew it wasn't. Michael and Roxy had a child together. That was a bond not easily forgotten.

I would like to say it wouldn't change our budding relationship. But I knew that Michael had loved Roxy. I knew when she left that it had changed the course of his life.

One of Michael's close friends had once told me how loyal Michael was. That once he let someone into his circle—which he rarely did—that person stayed there. He or she was a friend for life.

I shook my head, trying to sort out my thoughts but knowing this wasn't the time or place.

"What do you think, Elliot?" Chloe stared up at me, waiting for me to respond.

I realized I hadn't even heard her question, and guilt flooded me. "What was that, sweetie?"

"I said, what do you think of Pomeranians? That's what I want. A cute little Pomeranian I can name Fluffy. Do you think my dad will ever go for it?"

I forced a smile, even though it took entirely too much energy. "I don't know. You'll have to talk to your dad about that."

She peered over my shoulder. "How much longer do you think he's going to be talking to that woman?"

"I have no idea. Maybe they have a lot to catch up on." I almost felt sick to my stomach as I said the words.

Worst-case scenarios went through my mind. I didn't generally consider myself a pessimist, but, right now, that's exactly how I felt. Pessimistic. Like something was on the verge of changing. Like just when this one thing in my life had started going right, something was bound to come in and make everything go wrong.

That seemed to be the way my life operated lately.

A moment later, someone cleared his throat behind

me. I turned and saw Michael standing there, his expression pinched. "Elliot, could I talk to you for a minute?"

I nodded and stood from the table, abandoning my cold pizza. "Of course."

He glanced to Chloe. "You stay there. Finish your dinner. I'll be back in a minute."

But as Michael and I stepped away, I couldn't deny that dread pooled in my stomach.

CHAPTER EIGHT

AS MICHAEL LED me into the living room, I glanced toward the front door. Roxy still stood there, nibbling on her fingernail with her shoulders hunched as if in distress. I expected her to glance up at us, but she didn't.

However, the fact that she was still here spoke volumes.

Once in the living room, Michael didn't bother to sit down. He paused in the middle of the space, looking too wired to even attempt to be seated.

He kept his hand on my arm as he leaned toward me and lowered his voice. "Roxy is back."

I swallowed hard and nodded. "I gathered that. What are you going to do?"

He stepped away from me and ran his hand through his hair before placing his hat back on it. I'd never seen

Michael look so flustered before. He was usually calm and cool.

"I have no idea," he muttered before dragging his gaze back up to mine. "She wants to see Chloe."

My eyes widened. There were so many implications to that. I didn't even know what kind of advice to give him. "Are you going to let that happen?"

"Chloe has been talking about her mom nonstop since she learned to say her first word. I don't want to keep them apart."

I understood what he was saying but . . . "What if she leaves again?"

"Exactly. I don't want Chloe to get hurt." Michael let out a long breath and turned away again. "This wasn't supposed to happen."

I saw the agony on his face, the pull between two choices and the implications of each one. It was like a fraying piece of fabric being pulled further apart, leaving only a single thread—a tightrope, of sorts. Navigating the narrow line was treacherous.

"I know you'll make the right choice, Michael."

His gaze met mine again, still unsteady. "I'm going to have to let them meet each other. It would be a big mistake to keep them apart. I don't know if Chloe would ever forgive me for it."

I couldn't argue with his statement, though I knew it was complicated. Michael had to do what was best for his daughter and consider both the long-term and short-term consequences.

I leaned closer, another question on my mind. "Why is Roxy back, Michael? Why now?"

"She said she had a wakeup call, and she wants to make things right."

Before we could say anything else, a voice sounded behind us.

"Mom?"

I sucked in a breath and turned, all my questions fading as reality took center stage.

Chloe stood in the entryway, her eyes wide and hopeful as she stared at the woman by the door.

The next instant, she darted toward Roxy.

Based on everything I witnessed, Chloe and her mom had reunited—for better or for worse.

"I THINK about you all the time, Mommy." Chloe sat in Roxy's lap and twirled the woman's hair between her fingers as she stared up in adoration at her mother.

"Oh, baby, I think about you all the time too." Roxy kissed the top of Chloe's head, her features softening with unshed tears. The woman's blonde hair fell across her face as she leaned closer to her daughter, looking like she never wanted to let her go.

The bond between the two had been instantaneous.

I didn't want to admit that I felt a stab of jealousy. But I did.

I chided myself for the emotion. I should be happy that the girl had been reunited with her mother. And I was. But I'd enjoyed the special connection Chloe and I had. Somehow, I wondered if this sudden reappearance of her biological mother might erase it.

It didn't matter right now.

There were other things at play, and those were the issues we needed to concentrate on. To think about my own problems would be selfish.

"Mommy, why did you come back?" Chloe looked up at Roxy.

Michael and I were seated across from them, watching the two of them interact on the couch. Michael felt cagy beside me, like he wanted to spring up, take Chloe into his arms, and whisk her away somewhere where she would never get hurt.

It was too late for that. Well, maybe not literally. But Chloe might never forgive him if he did that.

"It's a long story, sweetie." Roxy rubbed Chloe's hair back from her face. "Just know that I've missed you so much. I've thought about you every day."

"I've missed you too, Mommy. I'm so glad you're here now. I knew you'd come back one day. I knew it!"

Roxy smiled softly before glancing at Michael. "I was

hoping that the three of us might be able to spend some time together. We have some catching up to do."

I got that message loud and clear. Roxy wanted me to leave.

And that took a lot of nerve.

Yet, at the same time, part of me also wanted to leave. I felt like I was interrupting a moment I wasn't meant to be a part of. My relationship with Michael was way too new for me to play any role in this discussion.

With that thought settled, I stood. "You know what? I should go. I want to get a jump start on my work for tomorrow anyway."

Michael stood beside me and reached for me, but I stepped out of the way. I didn't want him to talk me out of this.

"Elliot . . ." he murmured.

"No, really. I'm good." I sent him a look, trying to communicate all the things I couldn't say out loud. But the tortured look in his eyes told me that wasn't enough. Instead, I finally said, "Walk me to my car?"

Michael glanced at Chloe before nodding. I started toward the front door when Chloe popped out of Roxy's lap and threw her arms around my waist.

"Thank you for coming over tonight, Elliot," she rushed. "It was fun. Can we do it again sometime?"

"I would love to do it again sometime." I rubbed her back one last time and stole another glance at Roxy, who stared at us with a strange look in her eyes. Was that resentment? Disdain? I wasn't sure.

Michael placed his hand on the small of my back and led me to the front door. We walked silently, and each of my steps felt like they took twice the effort necessary.

As soon as we stepped outside, Michael turned toward me. He almost seemed to age before my eyes. His features looked heavier, more burdened. It was almost like his boat had been swept out to sea and left him treading treacherous waters. It was a Yerbian expression.

"I feel like I'm in way over my head right now," he muttered.

I rested my hand on his chest and felt his heart pounding beneath my palm. "You're a good dad. Trust your instincts. You'll make good choices. I have faith in you."

Half of his lip tugged up in a smile, and he took my hand, kissing the top of it. "Thank you for believing in me, Elliot."

"Of course. That's a no-brainer, as my sister would say."

His smile widened just a bit more. "You're learning some Americanisms."

"Slowly but surely." My smile slipped. "I'll be praying for you."

"I can use all the prayer I can get right now." After a

resigned sigh, Michael leaned toward me and brushed his lips against my cheek. "I'll talk to you later, okay?"

I nodded, realizing this day hadn't gone anything like I'd planned. "Sounds good."

But as I walked out toward my car, I couldn't help but think that I was closing the door on some kind of chapter of my life—a chapter I'd only begun to explore.

CHAPTER NINE

I WAS STILL REELING as I left Michael's house. I couldn't stop thinking about Chloe sitting in Roxy's lap and looking so comfortable, so content.

Then my mind bounced to the image of Michael, Roxy, and Chloe together.

As a family.

As it should be.

My heart twisted at the image.

I knew I needed to stop dwelling on it, to stop torturing myself with the thoughts. But I couldn't seem to do that.

I gripped my steering wheel a little too tightly as I headed down the road.

I should go home. It was getting late. But the last

thing I wanted to do was to sit around doing nothing. Then I definitely *would* be thinking about the what ifs.

My mind drifted to Velma instead. I remembered the list of people I'd talked to today at Velma's apartment complex. Several people hadn't been home. In fact, those residents had probably been at work. But what if they were back now?

I glanced at the time. It was only seven thirty, and it was still daylight outside.

On a whim, I turned toward Velma's place. Maybe I could talk to a few more people and get some more answers tonight.

The best thing I could do was to focus all my attention on this investigation. A person's thought life could become a slippery slope. That's what my father had always told me. *As the mind thinks, the body acts.*

That's why I was going to keep my thoughts focused on finding Velma and not on Michael and Roxy and whatever might be happening right now at his place.

It wasn't that I didn't trust him. I did. The situation was just complicated.

Enough said.

Several minutes later, I pulled into Velma's complex. I parked my car in the lot and climbed out. Instead of rushing toward the residences, I leaned against my sedan for a moment and stared at the place.

I imagined Velma getting back from her friend's

house. It would have been dark that time of night. I pictured her climbing out of her car as I'd just done. I imagined her starting toward her apartment.

What had happened in the meantime? Had someone knocked her out? Used a stun gun? Chloroform? Did people really use those things in real life?

I had no idea.

Had Velma felt a rush of terror? People said your life flashed before your eyes. Was that what had happened?

I didn't know, but none of the scenarios that went through my mind brought me any comfort.

I needed to talk to more people. I needed to do everything I could to find my friend.

But before I headed toward the apartment complex, I heard a sound behind me. My entire body tensed as I anticipated trouble.

Maybe I shouldn't have ever come here alone.

———

I TWIRLED AROUND, ready to fight, fists raised in the air.

But all the air left my lungs when I spotted the figure behind me.

Dylan Hunter.

I lowered my arms and sagged against the car, relief rushing through me. It wasn't anyone dangerous.

Thank goodness.

"I didn't mean to scare you." He frowned apologetically. "I was about to say your name when you turned."

I didn't doubt his words were true. "What are you doing here?"

Hunter eyed me. "I might ask you the same question."

"I'm trying to talk to everybody at the apartment complex to find out if anyone saw anything," I admitted. "You?"

He crossed his arms, his protective walls popping back up. "Even though the FBI has officially taken over this case, I'm trying to picture what may have played out last night. Watching for anything specific to this area. Trying to get a feel for this investigation."

I nodded and felt my throat tighten as the reality of what had happened hit me once again. "I can't believe Velma's gone."

Hunter's jaw tightened. "I know. This guy is getting braver. He's not leaving as much time between his abductions. I don't like to think that he's escalating, but he seems to be."

"What does that mean for Velma? That she'll die sooner rather than later?" I felt sick to my stomach as the words left my lips. But I had to know.

"We don't know. Like I said before, in the past this guy has generally kept his victims alive for at least two weeks. Sometimes, I'm not sure if it's a good or a bad thing."

"Because we don't know what's happening to them in the process," I finished.

"We do know there are no signs he tortured his victims, though. I suppose that's something to be thankful for." Hunter's words sounded lackluster, like he wanted to believe them but couldn't quite do so.

I studied Hunter's face for a moment, contemplating my next question before I spoke. His features all seemed so tight, so melancholy and even distant. "So, have you seen anything out of the ordinary tonight?"

"No, I haven't. And you shouldn't be out here alone now."

"The Beltway Killer just struck," I said. "It's not like he's going to strike again the next day."

"You and I both know that there's more at stake here." Hunter leveled his gaze at me as if challenging me to look away.

Not long ago, I'd told him about my father and my suspicion that his death hadn't been natural causes like officials had claimed. I couldn't deny Hunter's statement. The stakes had never been higher.

"I know," I said. "There is a lot at stake. But I can't stop pursuing the truth just because of fear."

Hunter stepped closer, a new emotion crossing his gaze. "Maybe you are just like me."

I raised my chin, wondering what he was referring to. The look in his eyes caused my lungs to freeze. We shared a connection—a connection borne of loss and grief. Those emotions could bond people quickly, deeply.

"I can't make sense of my own life," he said. "But when I can put together the pieces of tragedy for somebody else, it makes me feel a lot better about myself and my situation. It gives me hope."

My heart pounded into my chest. Hunter had nailed it. That was one of the reasons I loved being a PI so much. I loved it when things made sense. When they fit.

That didn't always happen in life. But when you could open and close an investigation . . . the satisfaction was unbelievable.

Something passed between Hunter and me, and I cringed. I wasn't sure how to bring up the fact that Michael and I were together since Hunter and I weren't actually dating either. It was all a confusing mess, and I was definitely no relationship expert.

But I remembered why I'd been drawn to him. He was smart, kind, and wounded. Those wounds had ultimately kept us apart.

Hunter stared at me another moment before nodding at the apartment complex behind me. "Who do you need to talk to?"

There it was again. Hunter's ability to quickly get close and to quickly distance himself. Would he ever let anyone beyond his walls again?

I put the question aside and held up my list. "I have at

least six people on the second floor who weren't home when I came by earlier."

Hunter nodded. "I'll go with you to talk to them. Unofficially."

"You don't have to do that. I know you have other things to do." One part of me didn't want to keep him from his work. Another part of me felt freer to speak with people without his supervision.

He put his hand on my back and led me toward the complex. "I don't mind. I'd feel better knowing that you were safe."

I almost roared that I was independent and that I could take care of myself. But I knew that was a fallacy. It didn't matter if you were male or female, strong or weak, rich or poor. We all needed people to look out for us.

Living here in Storm River had proven just that.

CHAPTER TEN

AN HOUR LATER, I left the complex.

Hunter had faithfully stayed beside me as I questioned the residents. But no one had seen anything. I supposed I shouldn't be surprised.

There was only one more person I needed to talk to on the second floor. Everybody else was accounted for. I knew Oscar and Michael also needed to talk to a few people, but I didn't know which apartments those were. I would need to leave that task to my boss and colleague.

Hunter had walked me back to my car and made sure I was snugly inside. He continued to wait there until I drove away.

Meanwhile, he remained at the apartment complex. No doubt he was going to stay there and look for any other clues he may have missed.

I appreciated his dedication to the case. I wished I could stay and do more also, but I sensed he wanted me to leave. It was just as well. I needed to get home and check on my mom and my sister.

When I walked into my house, my mom and Ruth greeted me from the kitchen table, where they sat together over tea. But, of course, the first thing they noticed was that I wasn't acting like myself.

"You must have had a rough day." Ruth squinted as she scrutinized me.

I glanced at them a moment. The two of them appeared to be catching up with each other after busy days. My heart panged with grief for a moment. I missed those moments of normalcy. Moments when I felt like my life would continue forward as expected. In Yerba. With my mom, dad, and sister. Listening to the sounds of the rainforest in the morning and picking fresh fruit for snacks.

You truly didn't know how good you had it until that good disappeared.

Were those good moments still there? Was I avoiding them? In denial?

I wasn't sure.

Before I could respond to my sister, a coughing fit overtook her.

More concern rose in me. My sister had cystic fibrosis, a lung disease. She needed a double lung transplant, and she needed it soon. She was on the transplant list and steadily moving up. But we still needed the money to make sure that this surgery happened.

The hospital doing the transplant required a verification of the funds—not only for the surgery itself but for the $2,500-a-month anti-rejection drug that my sister would have to take for the rest of her life.

"It's been one of those days," I admitted.

It was one of the few truly honest things I'd said to my family in a while. Not that I lied to them. I just tried to keep certain facts quiet—facts that might worry them.

Like the fact that somebody was trying to kill me. That my father might have been murdered. That his killer might possibly be watching me now. That my father was a spy.

So many things.

I figured that my mom and sister had enough on their shoulders without me adding to their concerns.

But I knew right now that there was no getting around the truth about why I looked like I'd been wrapped around a tree twice and then slung back again.

"Let me fix you a cup of tea." My mom rose and started toward the kettle on the stove. "Then you can tell us about your day."

I smiled. I needed to open up to Mama more than I did. We'd been so close while I was growing up. But then I'd hit my teenage years. That was followed by hiding my engagement from her. After that ended, my family had escaped halfway across the world to this new home.

Put all those events together, and walls had been erected that hadn't been there before.

I hadn't even realized it until lately, but those barriers were definitely there. My mom was reaching out, and I seemed to keep pushing her away.

Was I becoming like Hunter?

As my mom fixed my tea, Ruth stared at me from across the table. She was in high school, and she had adjusted to American life a little too easily it seemed sometimes. She had street smarts that I'd never had, and she could read me like a book. The problem was, I didn't want to be read.

"What's going on?" Ruth still eyed me with a bit of skepticism.

"I'll just wait for Mama before I say anything."

Finally, my mom sat back down across from us, and I took a sip of lavender tea. It was the perfect drink before bedtime.

My mom and sister silently waited for me to start.

I cleared my throat before saying, "My coworker disappeared."

My mom gasped. "Disappeared?"

I nodded, but my head felt like it weighed two hundred pounds as I did so. "They think it may have been . . . the Beltway Killer."

My sister's hand fell from where it had been resting near her neck and hit the table. "What?"

"It's true," I said. "We've spent all day trying to track her down."

Mama stood, her nostrils flaring. "Elliot Maria Ransom, I forbid you."

That had *not* been the response that I had been expecting. Had I heard her correctly? Maybe I was too tired to interpret her tone.

"What?" I finally asked when she didn't explain.

Her finger went into the air—a sure sign she was dead serious about this. "The last thing I need is for you to be chasing some serial killer."

"I'm hardly chasing a serial killer," I explained, trying to keep the exasperation out of my voice. "I'm simply looking for my friend."

"You can't get wrapped up in that. What if something happens to you?"

"It's not like I'm chasing him down alone. Michael is with me."

Her eyes narrowed. "Yes, Michael. Let's talk about Michael."

More tension built in my chest until I felt like I wanted to explode. I reminded myself to stay cool, though. High emotions wouldn't help this situation. "What about Michael?"

"What's going on between the two of you?" Mama

continued. Though she wasn't Hispanic, I almost thought I heard an accent in her voice now. "And what about that Hunter guy? I thought the two of you were starting to date. Now all I hear about is Michael. You get that dopey smile on your face when you talk about him."

I let out a long breath, and, like uncountable times today, I just wanted to disappear. Too bad that wasn't an option right now.

"I'm just trying to figure things out." I tried to keep my voice steady. "Michael and I are friends. Maybe more."

"And Hunter?" She continued to stare at me like only a mother could do—hand on hip and foot tapping the floor.

I shrugged and looked at my sister, pleading for her to cause some type of interruption or something.

She didn't. Instead, she stared at me, waiting for me to respond.

I cringed, feeling like I'd been tied to a pole in front of interrogators holding their bows and arrows.

"It's all confusing," I finally said. "But my love life is the least of my worries right now. Finding Velma is my top priority."

"I'm sorry to hear about your friend," Mama continued. "But you have no business sticking your nose into this investigation. You're going to get yourself killed."

The way she looked at me with such stubborn determination in her eyes made me wonder if she and my father had conversations like this in the past. What if she'd known Papa was a spy? I'd just assumed she'd been in the dark and that, like me, she'd believed my father simply worked for the government.

But what if that wasn't the case at all?

"Elliot, you've got to promise me that you are not going to get involved in this." My mom stared me in the eye, waiting for my response.

My lungs tightened. This was *not* a position I wanted to be in. I didn't want to lie to my mom. But I couldn't let my friend die at the hands of a serial killer either.

"I can't promise you that, Mama."

"Elliot . . ." Warning strained her voice.

"I'm sorry, Mama. You know I want nothing more than to please you. But this is my friend we're talking about."

"And this is my family I'm talking about!" Her voice rose with each syllable, and her cheeks reddened.

I wasn't sure I'd ever heard my mom raise her voice before. It sent a shock through me and made me feel like I couldn't breathe.

And I didn't like it.

I stood, my chair screeching across the floor. "You know what? I don't really think I want this tea after all. I think I'm just going to go to bed."

"Elliot . . ." Mama's voice trailed with admonition.

But there was nothing else I could say to her. There

was no way I could convince her that investigating was the right thing.

Instead, I escaped into my bedroom and found the journal my father had left me. I prayed that he had some words of wisdom for me there, that he could reach me even beyond the grave and give me some guidance on how I should proceed with my life.

Because I felt lost right now.

CHAPTER ELEVEN

WHEN I CAME into the office the next morning and saw Velma's empty desk, reminders of what had happened hit me again and again.

I just couldn't believe that she was gone. That the Beltway Killer might have taken her.

On top of that, I had no idea what had transpired last night between Michael and Roxy.

The unknowns set me on edge—had me jumping at sounds and snapping at people. I didn't even feel like rhyming about anything, which never happened.

You know why that was? Because I felt like life had no rhyme or reason right now. All the awful poetry I could mentally write wouldn't change that.

However, I had found some advice in my father's

journal last night. He'd written, *Do the right thing, even when it feels wrong.*

He'd probably had no idea just how much those words meant to me now.

Oscar was in his office—I saw him through the open door—but he seemed preoccupied with something. Instead of talking to him, I went straight to my desk.

I'd hardly been able to sleep all night, so I'd spent most of my time researching the Beltway Killer. I'd put together a timeline. Organized a dossier of the victims. I'd even put together my own criminal profile. Granted, I had no education on how to do so. I purely went off gut instincts.

As soon as Michael got into the office, I'd share what I had put together and get everyone's feedback on it.

Michael dragged himself into the office a few minutes after I arrived. I couldn't help but notice he looked tired. Maybe even a little anxious, based on his gaze. It was usually steady; today it wasn't.

He waved at Oscar before walking into the office and staring at me for a minute. Something unspoken lingered in his gaze.

"Elliot." His voice sounded crisp.

I knew there was more he wanted to say, but he couldn't. We couldn't risk Oscar overhearing anything personal. That meant I would need to wait.

"How are you?" I asked. But what I really wanted to

know was how things had gone with Roxy. I wanted details. Information. A promise that everything would be okay.

God was the only one who could promise me that, though. And His answer might not include anything this side of heaven.

"We should probably talk—" he started.

Before he could finish, Oscar bellowed from his office, "I want to see the two of you in here. Now."

It looked like our conversation would have to wait until later. But the ominous tone to Michael's voice set me on edge. What had happened last night? Whatever it was, it had Michael apprehensive.

I grabbed the folder I'd put together and followed Michael into Oscar's office.

I paused just inside the doorway and observed my boss. Oscar didn't look like he had gotten much sleep either, with his rumpled clothing and the circles beneath his eyes. I wasn't sure what he'd been doing, but it appeared we were all worried about Velma.

It was nice to know that Oscar had a heart.

"Any updates?" Michael stepped closer to Oscar's desk.

Oscar frowned and rolled a pen between his fingers.

"Not that I've heard. I checked in with a contact at the police station this morning, but he was tight-lipped." Oscar put his pen down and sighed. "This case really has me stumped. There's nothing to point to who this killer may be or where Velma is."

I cleared my throat, my lungs deflating. However, I had to remember the work I'd done last night. "I'm no expert, but I have a few ideas."

Michael and Oscar both stared at me.

I opened my folder. "I did some research on the psychology of a killer. I know I'm an amateur, but I put together a profile."

I handed both Michael and Oscar paper packets and gave them a moment to study what I'd compiled. I held my breath, waiting for their reactions.

Finally, they both looked up and nodded.

"Impressive," Oscar muttered.

I relaxed slightly. "Thank you."

"So you think this killer is someone on the younger side—" Michael started.

"Younger being late twenties, thirties, maybe even forties," I said. "There's really not enough information to go on yet. But that's the information that was on the flyer the police put out. Someone must have thought they saw this man at some point if the police are using those details."

"I believe that information came from a supposed witness who saw the third victim before she disappeared," Oscar said. "But the details were all hazy and uncertain."

"What else?" Michael continued, his gaze on me instead of the dossier.

"There were no drag marks on the victims," I explained. "That probably means they were carried to the places where they were found. That would require some strength."

"So he was organized and meticulous," Oscar said.

"Exactly." I liked it when people saw things as I did. "And he hasn't been caught yet, so he must be relatively smart and have the ability to focus on details."

"True." Michael nodded slowly.

"He has the inability to form deep relationships," I continued. "In my estimation, at least."

Oscar twisted his thick head. "Where did you get that fact from?"

"No one he knows has come forward with information on him," I said. "He's probably private. Maybe he was even rejected, and, because of that, he's looking for affirmation outside his social circle. Maybe that's why he keeps his victims for so long. They fill some kind of need in him."

When I finished, I noticed Michael and Oscar still staring at me with a halfway bewildered look in their gazes.

I cringed. Had I overstepped? Was I totally off base?

I waited for their reaction, the seconds dragging on. I had no choice but to sit there with my chin up.

"Good job, Elliot." Oscar nodded, something close to admiration in his gaze.

I sucked in a breath. Had he just given me affirmation? I could hardly believe it.

Oscar wasn't that type.

"Thank you," I finally said, nearly choking on the words.

"I agree," Michael said. "You did some good work, Elliot."

"I also put together dossiers on the victims and compiled all the old news articles I could find on the killings. I thought it might help to have everything spelled out and in front of us." I handed them those papers also.

"Impressive," Oscar muttered, glancing at them.

As Oscar's phone buzzed, he looked down and grunted.

A second later, he turned on the TV in the corner of his office. "That was a friend of mine. There's something on the news right now about Velma."

I held my breath as I waited to hear whatever was being reported.

I WAS SO ENTRANCED while watching the news feature on the Beltway Killer that I hardly heard someone step into the office. When I felt a shadow behind me, I nearly jumped out of my chair.

Hunter.

My heart crashed in my chest.

I quickly stood and met him in the doorway. "Hunter. I wasn't expecting to see you here."

His gaze looked haunted as he observed me. "I was hoping to ask you a few more questions about Velma."

"Of course," I murmured. "Whatever we can do to help find her."

Hunter briefly nodded at Oscar and Michael before following me into the reception area. Even out here, we heard the TV playing. Heard the report on the news.

The feature had mostly been a depressing update. The reporter informed viewers that the Beltway Killer had supposedly taken another victim. Velma's picture had flashed on the screen.

Seeing her photo on TV made my stomach squeeze with grief.

We had to find her.

"Do you want to talk to everybody or just me?" I asked.

Hunter took my arm and led me farther away from Oscar's office. "Just you. To start with, at least."

"Of course." I pointed to my office, and we both went in and sat down.

As we did, Hunter studied my face for a moment. "Are you hanging in?"

"Not really." There I went again, being honest. I was so used to covering my true feelings by saying that I was doing fine even when I wasn't. It felt like a shock when the truth actually left my lips.

"We're doing everything we can to find her," Hunter said. "I promise."

"But none of those other women were found alive," I reminded him, unable to keep the grim tone from my voice. "How are we going to find Velma in time?"

He let out a long breath, tension etched in the wrinkles on his forehead. "That's what I'm hoping you can help me with. I need more information about her and her habits. Even though I talked to a couple of Velma's friends from karaoke, it seems that nobody knows her very well. I'm hoping you can change that."

I shifted in my seat. "I'll share whatever I can. Of course."

Hunter nodded and looked down at his notebook. "We know that Velma grew up down in Georgia. She didn't have a lot of money. I suppose that's an understatement. Her family was actually homeless for a while."

"I didn't know that." I should have known, though. Why hadn't Velma and I ever talked about those things? But I supposed that explained why Velma was such a cheapskate. Growing up not having what you needed . . . you probably did whatever necessary to survive.

"Do you know why she came here to Storm River?" Hunter studied me, his gaze intense yet quietly unobtrusive.

I tried to recall everything she'd ever told me, which didn't seem like that much right now. "All I know is that Velma was in an abusive relationship. Oscar helped her to get away from her boyfriend and start a new life away from this guy. He hired her here to give her a start."

Hunter's eyebrows flickered up, as if that news surprised him. "I see. Does she ever talk about her friends or any other hobbies?"

I shook my head. "I didn't even know she liked karaoke."

Shame pressed on me at that thought. Why hadn't I known that?

I supposed it was because Velma and I mostly talked work when we were together. There was usually so much to talk about pertaining to our cases that we didn't need to get too personal. Maybe I was playing it safe myself. If I didn't ask Velma too many personal questions then maybe she wouldn't ask me many either.

But now I could see that was a mistake. I should have been working harder to develop more community.

"Have you found anything in your investigation, Elliot?" Hunter stared at me, as if daring me to keep something to myself. The intensity in his gaze actually set me back.

I shook my head. "I wish we had. It's hard to even know where to go. There are no clues."

Hunter slowly nodded. "Yeah, I get that. I'll talk to your . . . colleagues and see if they have anything to add."

My heart thumped into my chest. "Of course."

"It's no problem, Elliot." Hunter stared at me just a little too long, almost like he wanted to say something, but I wasn't sure what it was. "I'll talk to you later, okay?"

I nodded, probably a little too quickly. "That sounds great. Thanks again."

But I hated the awkwardness I felt with Hunter now. He was a good guy. We hadn't been on enough dates to be official. We hadn't been on enough dates that I should even feel this guilty.

But I did.

Guilt was just part of my emotional makeup, I supposed.

If only romance was my biggest worry right now.

CHAPTER TWELVE

I STARED at the information I'd compiled, hoping something would jump out at me.

It didn't.

Even detail-oriented people could slip up sometimes. Somewhere along the way this guy had to have made a mistake. We just had to find that mistake and exploit it.

After Hunter left, Michael wandered into the office, sat at his desk, and wheeled his chair toward me as I sat at my own desk. "Anything new?"

I shook my head. "I wish there was. It's almost like the victims were wiped clean before their bodies were left. As far as the police know, the killer hasn't left any evidence."

Michael frowned before grabbing some bouncy balls from his desk and beginning to juggle them. That's what he did when he needed to sort out his thoughts.

"That seems almost impossible, doesn't it?" he finally murmured.

I nodded. "It does. If only we could figure out where this guy is taking his victims before they die. Or find a car. Or find a witness to the crime. Something. *Anything.* I know Hunter wants to find this guy just as much as anybody. Maybe even more so."

"I'm sure." Michael caught all the bouncy balls in one hand and set them back on his desk.

"I, for one, can hardly stand just sitting in this office and not being out there actively looking."

Michael reached toward me and quickly squeezed my arm before withdrawing his hand. He lowered his voice as he said, "I know. It's hard. Oscar is going to talk to the various police municipalities in the cities where the victims were found."

"Sounds like a good place to start."

"I was thinking that maybe we could go to the sites where the bodies were left. Maybe there's some type of connection between those areas. I thought putting our eyes on them might help something click in place."

I nodded. It was worth a shot.

But I also sensed that Michael had things to tell me. Relational things. Roxy things.

Part of me dreaded hearing his update.

It didn't matter. I was a big girl. I could handle whatever was coming my way . . . I hoped.

MICHAEL and I decided to head toward the scene farthest away from Storm River. It was in an area of Northern Virginia called Tyson's Corner.

As Michael and I sat beside each other in his minivan, I decided not to bring up Roxy. Though I was dying to know what had happened last night, Michael should be the one to open up, and he seemed distracted.

Maybe he needed time. According to my GPS, this drive was going to take us almost an hour. I really hoped he wasn't silent on the subject the whole time.

Ten minutes into the drive, Michael rubbed his jaw, and I knew he was ready. His hands squeezed the steering wheel until white knuckles appeared.

"So, about last night . . ." he started.

I waited for him to continue.

"I had no idea that Roxy was going to show up." Michael's voice sounded strained, like this conversation had him twisted up inside.

I felt bad for him. I really did. But I was trying to give him his space so he could find the right words.

But his obvious struggle compelled me to say, "I bet that was a shock, especially since you haven't seen her for almost seven years, right?"

Michael nodded, but his eyes looked slightly glazed

as he stared at the road ahead. "That's an understatement."

When he didn't say anything for a moment, I again found the need to fill the silence—which I should have known was a bad idea.

"It seems like Chloe took right to her." The words burned as they left my lips. I was trying so hard to be level-headed here, but I'd be lying if I said the whole situation didn't leave me unsettled.

"Yeah, I can't believe it." Michael ran a hand over his face. "Chloe is smitten. She said she's been praying that her mom would come back, and now she has. She thinks this is a God thing."

Something about his words left me unsettled. "So what happened?"

"The three of us talked for a while after you left— mostly chitchat for Chloe's sake. When Chloe went to bed, Roxy and I had a chance to really talk."

Something about the way Michael said the words indicated there had been a big development. Maybe even something life-changing. That's what my instinct told me, at least.

"Did she have a good reason for being gone so long?" I held my breath as I waited for Michael's response.

"Actually, she did." He let out another long breath. "When she left Chloe with me, it was because she had a drug habit and knew she needed help. She realized she couldn't be a mom with those issues and checked herself in rehab. She said it was a really long journey."

I hadn't expected that one. "I see. But why didn't she just tell you? Why keep it a secret?"

Michael shrugged. "Shame? Embarrassment?"

"Then why stay away for seven years?" I didn't want to play devil's advocate here, but . . . I knew my questions were valid. Anyone who'd done what she'd done deserved a little scrutiny, at least.

"For the same reasons. She didn't think we'd forgive her or even that she deserved forgiveness, for that matter. She said she kept tabs on us and saw that we looked happy. She didn't want to mess things up between us."

"So why come back now?"

He rubbed his lips together and let out a long breath. As a car cut him off, he lay on his horn.

Very unlike Michael.

Was it this situation? Or the horribly bad traffic?

I knew what my bets were on.

"Last month, Roxy . . . she was diagnosed with a brain tumor. The doctors have only given her a few months to live."

I sucked in a breath. That was the last thing I'd expected to hear. "Wow. That's . . . terrible."

"I know."

I rubbed my throat, wishing it would stop burning.

"What happened after Roxy told you her story last night?"

Michael's jaw tightened. "She just got into town, so she stayed on my couch."

The burning in my throat turned into an all-out fire, so hot that I could hardly breathe. I hadn't expected that answer. And I didn't like it.

But how did I express that without sounding jealous or overbearing?

"Wow," I finally muttered. "That's . . . unexpected."

He glanced at me, his gaze pleading for understanding. "I didn't know what to do. I couldn't put the mother of my child out on the street."

"She doesn't have any money for a hotel?"

"No, she doesn't. She doesn't have anything right now."

That bad feeling in my gut continued to grow. "I see."

He pulled his eyes from the road for long enough to glance at me again. "Nothing happened between us, Elliot. It wasn't like that."

I shrugged, grateful that the heavy DC traffic kept me halfway distracted for a moment. "I didn't say anything happened."

"But I know this is all weird. It's weird for me. I don't exactly know how to handle the situation."

"It would be a lot for anyone to know how to handle." Then another thought slammed into my mind. Before I could stop it, the question escaped. "Is she at your place now?"

The lines on Michael's face deepened. "Unfortunately, she is."

I nodded slowly, unsure how I felt about that. But again, I reminded myself that Michael and I weren't far enough into our relationship for me to put my foot down. What was between us was too new, too fresh. Chloe didn't even know her father and I were dating.

Michael squeezed my hand. "I know this has to be awkward for you, Elliot. I'm really sorry that you're in the middle of all this."

"Maybe you'll finally get some of that closure that you've been looking for, at least."

"That would be a blessing that would come out of this, I suppose." His tone sounded unconvinced, however. He stared at the road ahead, a frown tugging at his lips.

"How long are you going to let her stay at your place?" I had to admit that was bothering me. I liked to be level-headed, but even I had my limits.

"I'm not sure. I'm trying to find somewhere else for her to stay. I just know that Chloe really wants to get to know her. The last thing I want is for Chloe's heart to be broken, and I'm not sure if I can trust Roxy or not. Those are all things that I need to figure out."

I tried to read between the lines. I was pretty sure

Michael was saying that he might need some space right now.

Which seemed like a shame since we had literally just gotten together a few days ago.

But I wasn't going to stand between Chloe and her dying mom. I couldn't live with myself if I did.

Always do the right thing, even when it feels wrong. My father's words echoed in my mind.

Oh, Papa . . . do I have to?

I knew the answer.

As I glanced at Michael, I had to wonder if he still had feelings for the woman. He'd said she was the mother of his child and that she would probably always have a special place in his heart. But was that place platonic? Or was the best thing for Chloe for Michael and Roxy to get back together?

I hated the thought of it.

Lord, what am I supposed to do? I've really got no clue. I'm not one to be a shrew. I could really use some help from You.

As much as it killed me to tell Michael this, I had no choice but to say what I was about to say. "Take all the time you need, Michael. I know you have things you need to figure out. And I don't fault you for that."

"Elliot, that's not what I'm saying—" He quickly glanced at me, tension snaking through his features.

I withdrew my hand from his. I hadn't even intended to—the reaction had been instinctual.

I stared at my arms a moment, wondering what to do with them. Finally, I hugged them across my chest.

But I could still feel the warmth of Michael's touch on my fingers.

And I missed it.

That realization made my heart lurch with enough force that I flinched.

I hadn't expected the reaction.

I hadn't expected this conversation, for that matter.

"Elliot . . ." Michael started. His voice almost sounded pleading—something I'd never heard from him before.

"I mean it, Michael. I'm not going to come between you and your family. Please don't put me in that position."

"But you're the one I care about."

"Roxy is the one that you had a baby with."

As my words rang out, we pulled up to the cemetery where Trisha had been found.

It was a perfect distraction from this awkward conversation.

CHAPTER THIRTEEN

MICHAEL and I found a parking space at a public lot and walked over to the cemetery where Trisha Thomas's body was found.

Trisha had been left on top of a grave. I'd researched the area and made a note of it on my phone so we could find the exact location. Michael and I wove between the tombstones in search of the spot.

I wanted to pretend like things were normal between us. But I felt the tension. I felt that something had changed after our conversation on the way here.

Pressure pushed on my heart. That was sadness, wasn't it?

I knew it was. The heaviness was a result of something good being over before it had really begun.

Was this entanglement between Michael and I over? I

couldn't be sure. I only knew that things had gotten a lot more complicated at Roxy's sudden appearance.

"Here it is." I pointed to a tombstone in the distance.

It read Edna Murphy. 1917–1991. Loving wife, mother, and grandmother. May her memory be eternal.

There was nothing else special, per se, about the tombstone—nothing that made it stand out from the others.

"Why did he choose this one?" Michael asked, as if reading my thoughts.

"Good question," I said. "I have no idea."

I took out my phone and snapped some pictures so I could remember all the details. Then I paused and glanced around to see if there was anything unique about this cemetery.

Overall, the site seemed ordinary. Large oak trees were scattered among the tombstones, and the whole place was situated on rolling hills. The grounds were immaculate and well-kept.

But nothing I saw offered any clues about why this location might be important.

"Do you think we came out here for nothing?" I glanced at Michael.

He shook his head, but his jaw looked tight. "I think it's good to see where this killer has been. To walk in his footsteps. To visualize him driving up in the middle of the night. There's no fence around the cemetery. He could have pulled up, lifted his victim from the trunk, and placed her here like a corpse—only on the ground instead of six feet under."

"How do you know that the victim was in the trunk?"

"If I remember correctly, there were some carpet fibers found on one of the victims. That information was released to the press, I believe."

I shuddered as I imagined it playing out. Had the killer chosen this location because there wasn't a fence? Or was there another reason?

I glanced around again. I didn't see anything that looked vaguely like a security camera or an overhead light. For that reason, this area was prime for a crime like this.

I stood there for another moment, giving my silent respects to Trisha. She deserved that, at least. And, while I was at it, I even tried to offer some respect for Edna. The notion just seemed appropriate for the moment.

After a few minutes of silence, Michael turned toward me. "You ready to go?"

I nodded. But I'd really hoped we'd find something that would offer some insight into this case. We weren't done yet . . . and I really hoped all of this wasn't for nothing.

OUR NEXT STOP took us down to the Fairfax area and another cemetery. It was almost like the killer had changed his MO after his first two victims. They'd been left at cemeteries, but the rest had not. I wasn't sure what had happened to change his mind or if the change had been this man's plan from the start.

This cemetery looked similar to the last, except for the small fence surrounding it. As soon as Michael and I pulled through the gate, I glanced around.

Were those security cameras on the light posts?

Maybe—just maybe—they held some type of clue.

I looked down at the information I'd brought with me and directed Michael to the right gravesite.

We stopped in front of another plot. This tombstone read: Kenneth Jenkins. 1964–2004. Beloved father, son, and friend. Once met, never forgotten.

The epitaph was beautiful. Who wouldn't want that to be said of them? I hoped that was the way I was living my life also—that I was making a difference to those I met.

Michael and I again stared at the little patch of grass by a tombstone.

Why had the killer chosen this location? It still made no sense. And I *hated* it when things didn't make sense.

"You're observant, Elliot." Michael glanced at me. "Anything strike you?"

"As in, hit me?"

"No, as in . . ." He pressed his lips together in thought. "As in, has anything stood out to you here?"

I shook my head, maybe a little too quickly. But I already knew that answer. "No. There's nothing. Maybe I'm losing my touch."

"Don't be silly. How many steps did we have to climb to get to this part of the cemetery?"

I shrugged, trying not to feel self-conscious. "Thirty-two," I finally said.

Yes, I liked counting things. I liked knowing things. I just tried not to hang out my freak flag for everyone to see all the time.

"How many security cameras?" Michael continued.

I cringed again. "Eight. One on each light post."

"You've got a gift. If anyone's going to notice something that's strange or out of place, it's going to be you."

"I appreciate your vote of confidence." I only wished there was a way to ensure I wasn't going to let him down —that I wouldn't let the victims of the Beltway Killer down.

Just as I said those words, a man wearing coveralls started toward us from atop the hill. The man was probably in his sixties with a long gray beard and weathered skin. His eyes, wrinkled at the edges, made me think of someone brimming with wisdom.

Could you do this job and not realize just how fragile and precious life was? I doubted it.

He paused a few feet away.

"Here because of the Beltway Killer?" His voice sounded thin and frail as he addressed us.

"I guess you get a lot of people coming out this way for that reason," Michael said.

"We do," the man said. "I suppose people are curious, even if that does sound morbid."

I stepped into the cool shade of the oak tree as I felt my skin heating in the sun. "Were you working here when the body was found?"

A frown tugged at his thin lips. "I was. I was the one who found her. I came in for my morning shift at six a.m. I walked around the cemetery, just to make sure everything was okay, as I do every morning. To my surprise, I saw someone lying there." He shook his head, as if reliving the bad memories pained him. "I couldn't believe it. Never seen anything like that in my lifetime."

"I heard the victim looked peaceful," I said, remembering everything I'd researched. "That there were no cuts or bruises or anything wrong with her."

"That's right. This woman . . . her hair looked nice. Her clothes were clean. She may have even had a little bit of lipstick on."

I shuddered at the irony of death and beauty mingling together. It didn't seem right.

"A rose with a rope knotted around it was left on her chest. Never did hear that on the police reports, but I'm guessing the killer did this for all his victims. He wanted credit where credit was due. That was my impression, at least."

Why would anyone want credit for something like that? Then again, maybe there were some people who just wanted credit for *something*. Maybe the Beltway Killer felt like this was an accomplishment. Maybe he felt like the fact that the police hadn't caught him yet was something he was proud of.

I shuddered again. I couldn't imagine it at all. Maybe I didn't want to.

"What about the security cameras?" Michael continued. "Did they pick up anything?"

The man frowned as he glanced up at one of the devices near us. "None of them work. I don't usually tell people that, but they're mostly there just to scare people away."

Well, that was a letdown.

"We don't really have much crime here," the groundskeeper continued. "It's generally safe, except for the occasional troublemaker."

Again, I tried to picture the scene. If the killer hadn't been able to drive up to this area in the middle of the night, did that mean he'd parked, somehow got his victim around the gate, and carried her up these thirty-two steps to this very grave?

That was a lot riskier than simply driving up in the

dark. Was he getting braver? Did he want to take more risks with each new kill?

"Were there tire tracks by the gate?" I asked. "Do you remember?"

"Actually, the gate wasn't locked. From what I overheard the police saying, they think this guy drove up and left that poor woman on this grave."

I was getting a better picture in my mind just how this killer operated.

And I didn't like the images that came together.

CHAPTER FOURTEEN

MICHAEL and I visited the three other secondary crime scenes before heading back toward Storm River.

Our little town was where the final victim had been left. She'd been found on a hiking path along the river.

What was special about each location? I had no idea. Aside from the first two, each scene was different with no obvious links.

Though it was getting late, Michael and I decided to go back to the apartment complex and see if we could talk to anybody else who was there. As we drove, we mostly talked about the case. Maybe it was better that way.

When we got closer to the complex, I told him, "I came back here last night and talked to some of the residents I wasn't able to catch earlier during the day."

Michael did a double take at me. "You came back here by yourself? After everything that's been going on?"

"It was fine. Hunter was here."

Michael did another double take. "You and Hunter talked to people together?"

"It just happened to all work out." Was that a touch of jealousy in his voice? I couldn't be sure. It didn't matter. "Either way, everyone I talked to knew nothing. It was practically a waste of time, except for the fact that I crossed a few more people off my list. And I *love* crossing things off lists."

"Well, maybe we'll hit the jackpot tonight." But as Michael said the words, there was a new stiffness to his jaw.

I wasn't going to overanalyze the action. I had too many other things on my mind right now.

We got to the complex, and Michael came with me as I pounded on the door of the one person I hadn't been able to get in touch with the day before. To my surprise, someone answered—a man in his fifties with dark skin and a salt-and-pepper goatee.

He stared at Michael and me suspiciously, not saying anything.

"Hi there," I started. "I'm Elliot, and this is Michael. We're private investigators. A woman disappeared from this complex two nights ago, and we were hoping to ask you a few questions."

I had my spiel worked out. I should. I'd said it enough times already.

"What do you need to know?" The man didn't sound especially friendly or ready to open up.

I didn't let that stop me. "I was wondering if you happened to see anything strange going on in the parking lot two nights ago around ten thirty?"

The man grunted. "What do you mean?"

I narrowed my eyes, slightly confused about his confusion. "Did you know that somebody was abducted from this complex?"

He rubbed his goatee. "I got back into town about thirty minutes ago. I went up to Baltimore to see my son, and I just got home. What are you talking about?"

"I'm just curious, sir, but when did you leave for your trip?" Michael asked.

"Yesterday morning around five a.m. I was hoping to miss some of the traffic." He shifted. "Now, what's going on?"

Michael and I exchanged a glance. He gave me a subtle nod, silently telling me to take the lead on this one.

"A woman from this apartment complex went missing two nights ago," I started. "The police suspect it may be the work of the Beltway Killer, and we're trying to track down any information that might help us to find her. I take it you haven't talked to the police yet?"

"Like I said, I just got back to town. I haven't been

watching the news. Besides, I just moved into this complex a couple weeks ago. Don't know anyone here well enough yet for them to report any news to me. I'm sorry to hear that somebody else was taken." The man's shoulders seemed to loosen, like he no longer suspected us of being up to no good.

"We believe this woman got back to the apartment complex around ten thirty or eleven on Sunday night after being with her friends," I said. "We're looking for anybody who might have seen anything happening."

"What does your friend look like?"

I pulled out my phone and found Velma's picture—I'd taken it from her social media. As soon as I caught a glimpse of Velma's smiling face with her curly blonde hair and big earrings, my heart pounded with another moment of grief. I prayed desperately that she was okay.

The man studied it for a minute before nodding. "I do think I've seen her before. She lives on this floor, if I remember correctly."

I nodded. That was a good sign that he recognized her, at least.

"Did you happen to be outside or glance out your window anytime on Sunday night?" Michael asked.

"Funny that you ask. I was considering loading up my car that evening before my trip. But I glanced out my window and saw it was starting to rain, so I decided to wait."

"When you glanced out the window, did you see anything else?" I held my breath, desperately praying he might have an answer.

"As a matter of fact, I did see something."

I drew in a sharp breath. Could this be it? The lead we'd been waiting for?

"What did you see?" Michael asked.

"I saw somebody who might have been your friend, I suppose," he said. "Like I said, it was dark outside and hard to tell. But I'm pretty sure the woman I saw had a ponytail on the top of her head and curly hair. She was standing near a dark blue sedan. Maybe it was black."

Excitement lit in me. "What was she doing?"

"If I remember correctly, she got out of her car, and a man approached her. The two of them started talking. Didn't look like anything tense or suspicious. I figured they were friends."

"And what then?" I prayed that this man had kept watching and had seen something else.

"Then they walked together across the parking lot."

"Not toward the apartments?" Michael clarified.

"No, it almost looked like they were walking to his car."

"And she didn't appear to be in distress?" I asked as a mental picture began playing out in my mind.

"No. Not at all. I didn't see any signs of struggle or I

would have stepped in. I figured, like I said, that they were just two friends."

Michael stepped closer. "Was there anything distinct about the man that you remember?"

"I wish I could tell you more." The man shook his head, a grim expression lining his gaze. "But that's all. I'm sorry."

"You've been a huge help," I told him. "You're probably going to need to share with the police what you just told us."

"Of course. Whatever I can do."

At least we'd found something. I was grateful for each step forward . . . even if that step was a baby step.

MICHAEL and I didn't say anything until we climbed into his minivan. But my heart raced. We finally had some information we'd been searching for. Now we needed to figure out what to do with it.

"What are you thinking?" Michael turned toward me.

"A better image of this man is forming in my mind," I told him. "I just assumed that when he grabbed his victims that it was against their wills. But this changes everything."

Michael nodded. "This guy must be charming and have the ability to make people trust him."

"Most people don't trust strangers."

"What if he was a police officer?" Michael stared at me, watching for my reaction.

My heart thumped into my throat. "Do you mean like . . . Hunter?"

As soon as the words left my lips, my hand flew over my mouth. How could I have said that? Hunter's fiancée had died at the hands of this man. He was my friend.

Then again, Hunter did fit the description. That whole profile I'd given earlier today . . . I could have been describing him.

No, I was totally off base here. What was I thinking? I couldn't point at him as a serial killer.

"You really think Hunter would do something like this?" Michael asked.

I shook my head quickly and adamantly. "No, absolutely not. I don't know why I said his name."

Michael continued to stare at me. "Whether it's Hunter or someone else, whoever this man is, he obviously blends in. It's someone Velma thought she could trust. He must have lured her into his car and taken her. She probably didn't even know what she was getting into."

That sick feeling began to brew in my gut again. "You're probably right. We just need to figure out who that might be."

Silence fell between us, and we both seemed lost in our own thoughts.

We were going to wait here until the FBI arrived.

Or, to be more specific, until Hunter arrived. When we'd called to give him an update, he said he would come out also.

My gut twisted at the thought of Hunter. I couldn't believe I'd accused him of possibly being a killer. But the words had just slipped out.

I remembered Hunter's inability to get close. The way he had kissed me and apologized. How he'd held me at arm's length.

And then I also remembered his kindness. I mentally relived when he'd taken me to a bird sanctuary so I could feel a taste of home. I thought about the way he always checked on me to see how I was doing.

Then my mind went back again to the sometimes tortured look in his eyes. How he spent a lot of time alone on his boat. How I knew so very little about his past.

I shook my head again. I couldn't go there.

Then I knew it was too late.

I was already there.

I feared my friend might be guilty.

CHAPTER FIFTEEN

AS I LINGERED outside the apartment complex, watching as the FBI, along with Hunter, took a statement from the man that we'd talked to, someone new pulled onto the scene.

Kitty Kight. The intrepid reporter.

She glanced up at Hunter before her gaze met mine. As if making a split-second decision, she started toward me. Her ringlet curls bounced as she walked toward us, and her slim, fit figure moved effortlessly—almost like a puma stalking its prey.

"Fancy seeing you both here." She paused in front of Michael and me.

"How'd you know to come here?" I got right to the point.

I supposed that, if Hunter could be guilty, then

anyone could be guilty—including Kitty. I needed to keep my eyes wide open, and Kitty's appearance here was unexpected.

"I heard the call go out on my scanner," Kitty said. "I've been following the story of the Beltway Killer since it started. Whenever the police follow a lead, so do I."

"I thought you did community interest pieces, like on the charity softball game last weekend," I clarified. That had been my impression of the woman.

"That?" She shrugged. "I was filling in for another reporter who couldn't be there. But I normally work the crime beat. I thought you knew that."

I took note of that fact. It would have been good to know earlier.

"The police turned over some information to me about the Beltway Killer," Kitty continued. "I'm working on a big article about that now."

That's what Hunter had been talking about earlier when he'd mentioned giving the media some information. I tucked that data away also.

"So, do you guys know anything?" She glanced at me then Michael, waiting expectantly.

"No comment." Michael nudged himself in front of me, as he often did when he wanted to take the brunt of whatever might be coming toward us.

Chivalry. Personally, I loved it.

But it also reminded me that things were complicated

between the two of us right now. He was protective by nature. Not just of me, but of Chloe.

Maybe even of Roxy.

I frowned as soon as I remembered her, but I quickly tried to put that issue out of my mind for now. Priorities. Even my thought life needed to have them in place.

Especially my thought life.

"You know, we could work together to find this guy," Kitty suggested, raising her thin eyebrows in hopeful expectation. "Three heads are better than one, right?"

Michael shook his head, leaving no doubt where he stood. "Elliot and I work together—but we don't work with anyone else."

I hadn't expected him to be so defensive. Good. I appreciated his loyalty.

Kitty shrugged, seeming to brush off his response. "Have it your way then. It's too bad because you never know what kind of interesting stuff I might already know."

Now she did have my attention.

And I was sure that was exactly what she wanted.

"I guess I'll run along and talk to Hunter now." Kitty waved fingers in the air as if this was a laid-back social gathering. "Toodle-oo."

"Toodle-oo?" I looked back at Michael, wondering what in the world that meant.

"It's just a cutesy saying," Michael explained.

I should have known.

"You don't trust her?" I studied his face as I waited for his answer.

"Reporters are hard to trust. Besides, if Kitty's around, she might learn about Roxy being back in town. The last thing I want is my business all over the newspaper."

"She's a crime reporter. Why would she even care about something like that?"

Michael's gaze clouded. "In my experience, reporters just care about getting ahead. Telling something like that to her editor could gain personal bonus points. I don't want to offer her that opportunity."

I supposed that made sense. But I had to wonder if Kitty really knew anything . . . and if what she knew might outweigh the risk of Michael's privacy being invaded.

MICHAEL and I stayed at the apartment complex until Hunter finished talking to our witness.

Afterward, Hunter made his way toward us. His gaze looked hooded as he stopped a few feet away from Michael's minivan. "Thanks for sharing your information."

"Of course," I said, not liking the way the words caught in my throat.

But as I stared at Hunter, I couldn't help but think about the theory that had popped into my mind earlier. Could Dylan Hunter actually be the Beltway Killer?

On the surface, I thought the idea was ridiculous. But maybe I really should consider it. And maybe, while considering it, I would realize that it was totally inaccurate. Maybe if I examined the facts, the truth would become clear.

But for now, I had to admit that I felt hesitant as I talked to him.

"You guys staying here for any reason?" Hunter's somber tone remained.

Michael shrugged. "Just trying to get a feel for the crime scene."

Hunter nodded slowly, thoughtfully, as he usually did. "Okay."

As he reached forward to shake Michael's hand, he accidentally hit my phone and it tumbled from my grasp. Quickly, he picked it up and handed it back to me.

"Sorry about that," he muttered.

"No problem."

"Stay out of trouble," he cautioned before giving me one last lingering look and walking back to his unmarked sedan.

As he drove away, I turned and stared at the river in the distance, at the boats as they came and went. Anybody who was anyone in this area lived or worked on the water. Those of us who were in the peon class lived on the outskirts of town.

"I guess there's no reason for us to stay here much longer." Michael straightened, almost seeming hesitant to leave.

"Do you mind if we take a walk down by the docks?" I asked, an idea brewing in my mind.

"No, of course not."

I wasn't even sure exactly why I wanted to take a walk down there myself—except that I'd noticed some different boats here today than were here yesterday. So what if that meant there may have been some different boats here the night Velma was abducted as well?

I thought it was a possibility worth exploring, at least.

When Michael and I reached the water, its familiar scent rose up and wafted around us. Birds squawked as they perched on various pilings. A couple of people worked on their boats right there at the slip.

I slowed my steps and observed each of the vessels. I remembered what Michael had told me earlier about using my powers of observation. I couldn't be afraid of them or ashamed of them. I just needed to embrace them.

The first couple of boats we passed were on the smaller side. But, as I reached the end of the dock, I paused and stared at a sailboat. Was I looking at what I thought I was?

"Michael." I pointed at the boat. "That almost looks like a security camera, doesn't it?"

He stared in the direction I indicated before letting out a breath and nodding. "I think you're right. What do you say we go see if that captain is on board?"

CHAPTER SIXTEEN

"YEAH, I was here on Sunday night," Captain Cooke said as we stood on the slip beside his boat.

The man pulled out his phone as we waited to get more information from him. Cooke was probably in his seventies, with a thin build and weathered skin. He wore a floppy hat, boat shoes, and khaki shorts.

We'd asked him about the security camera, and now he was searching the footage on his cell. His words, his movements, his responses all seemed slow.

Or maybe I was just in a hurry for answers.

Either way, I needed to keep my impatience in check.

"I get so many notices about movement on my camera that I turned off the notifications," Cooke said, still staring at his phone screen. "I can check the past history, though."

Excitement raced through me. Maybe this was something.

We just needed a taste of the papaya to sustain us for a bit. We said that in Yerba when we talked about hope's power to carry us through difficult situations.

That was definitely how I felt now. I wanted just one bite of that papaya.

Cooke scrolled through a few things on his phone screen before letting out a grunt. "My camera did pick up on some kind of movement on Sunday evening. This says it was at 10:45. You can't see much." He squinted. "Just a license plate of a car driving away. Could be anybody, really."

"Do you mind if I look at that?" Michael reached for the phone in hopeful expectation.

"Not at all."

As Michael took the device from Cooke, I peered over Michael's shoulder so I could also see. Sure enough, you could see the shadow of a man and a woman getting into the car and then pulling away.

The timeline fit.

But, just as the captain had indicated, it was nearly impossible to make out any details.

I squinted.

But maybe, just maybe, I could make out that license plate.

"Can you freeze that frame?" I asked.

Michael hit Pause.

"Now see if you can blow it up," I said.

Using two fingers, Michael tried to enlarge the license plate. If I squinted, I could make out most of the numbers and letters, at least enough that I might be able to do some research.

It was something.

It was a taste of the papaya.

"Do you mind if I take a screenshot of this and send it to my phone?" Michael looked up at Cooke, waiting for his response.

"Knock yourself out," the man said.

Why would Michael want to knock himself out? The phrase made absolutely no sense to me. Another Americanism, no doubt.

Despite that, Michael took the screenshots. He was also able to forward the video to himself.

When he was done, I turned to him, another question lingering in my mind. "Does this mean we need to call Hunter again?"

This wasn't a competition. We all needed to work together, right? Velma's life was on the line here, after all.

"It's the responsible thing." Michael nodded before turning to the captain. "Will you be around for a while?"

"At least a couple hours."

Perfect.

I pulled out my phone and dialed Hunter's number. All I could think was: *Here we go again.*

————

MICHAEL and I went back to the office so we could research the license plate. As he did that, I brainstormed variations of the numbers and letters. The image had been blurry, so it was hard to be certain what the plate read.

If that was the killer's car, I was going to do everything within my power to figure out who owned it—especially if that meant finding Velma.

I was thankful that Michael had the means and know-how to run the plates. I supposed that was the advantage to becoming a licensed private investigator. He had access to official motor vehicle information that the average person didn't.

After several minutes of staring at his computer, Michael straightened, and I knew he'd discovered something.

I wheeled my chair toward him. Normally, I felt child-like whenever I let my chair glide across the floor. But there was nothing lighthearted about this moment. Too much was at stake.

"What is it?" I glanced at the screen.

"I got a hit on the license plate." Michael turned

toward me, his eyes bright with excitement. "It might be our first real lead."

"Who is it? What's his name?" I couldn't wait any longer. The suspense was killing me.

Michael's gaze met mine. "James Beasley."

I sucked in a breath. "James Beasley?"

Beasley had been the opposing team's coach at the softball game this past weekend, and he owned a sports equipment store in town.

Now that I thought about it, I *had* seen Beasley and Velma briefly talking at the game on Saturday. Plus, the rose with the nautical knot—the Beltway Killer's calling card—had been left in our dugout. Beasley could have easily done that, and no one would have batted an eyelash about seeing him there.

Could the killer have been in front of our eyes this whole time, and no one had seen him?

Michael and I needed to find out.

Michael's gaze met mine. "It looks like we need to go pay the coach a visit."

Before he even finished his sentence, I rose to my feet and grabbed my purse. There was no time to waste.

"Let's go," I said.

CHAPTER SEVENTEEN

"YOU KNOW the charity game is over," Beasley cackled as Michael and I walked into his store. "You come to gloat because you won?"

Michael strode toward Beasley, moving effortlessly through the wall-to-wall sports equipment. He had a hardness in his eyes that I'd rarely seen. "No, we're here to ask you a few questions about why you were at the Anchors Reach Apartments on Sunday evening."

Beasley's skin paled as he heard Michael's words. "Who says I was there?"

Michael paused in front of the cash register, his muscles bristling. "We have it on video. There's no need to play games. Tell us why you were there."

At Michael's harsh words, Beasley straightened from where he'd been leaning against the counter, and his muscles hardened as defensiveness crept in. "I don't have to tell you anything."

Michael leaned closer, undeterred by the bulky man. "You're right. You don't have to tell us anything, but you can be sure that you're going to need to have a little sit-down with the police."

Beasley blanched. "What are you talking about?"

"I'm talking about the fact that you were at that apartment complex at the same time the Beltway Killer's latest victim disappeared." Michael's hard stare locked onto Beasley. "And you fit the profile."

The coach quickly shook his head and raised his hands in the air. "I'm no Beltway Killer. I'm beginning to think you two just like to accuse me of murder."

"We're not joking, Beasley," Michael continued. "What were you doing at the apartment complex that night?"

Beasley's gaze darkened. "I was meeting someone. But I wasn't kidnapping her, and I definitely didn't kill anyone."

"We're going to need more details than that." I crossed my arms as I stood beside Michael. "Or we can take this up with the police. Your choice."

Beasley threw his hands in the air, obviously flustered at the accusations.

As he should be.

If Beasley had taken Velma, we needed to know as soon as possible. This was no time for niceties.

"Look, I met a lady a couple weeks ago and we began seeing each other. We've only been on about four dates. On Sunday evening at around ten thirty or eleven, I picked her up, and we went for a late-night drink. That was it."

I was going to need more details than that. "What's her name?"

"Lindsay Patterson," Beasley's voice cracked. "She lives at the apartment complex. You can ask her. But I definitely wasn't there to kill someone."

"We'll be talking to Lindsay," Michael said. "Because I don't believe in coincidences."

"This is one that you can believe in," Beasley said.

"I saw you talking to Velma at the game," I said. "What were you chatting about?"

"I told her I felt sorry for her because she worked with you guys." A satisfied smile flashed across his face before disappearing. "That's the truth."

"We'll be checking out your story." Michael raised his chin. "You can count on that."

Beasley's gaze narrowed. "I'm many things, but I am not a killer."

Maybe he was. Maybe he wasn't.

It looked like Michael and I had our first suspect.

"DO YOU BELIEVE HIM?" I asked Michael as soon as we climbed back into his minivan.

Michael rubbed his jaw as he started the engine, but he made no effort to leave. "We'll need to call Lindsay, of course. But I have to say it, I think Beasley is telling the truth. He's an arrogant jerk, but I don't see him as a murderer. Besides, the Beltway Killer seems to have more finesse. Beasley is like a bull in a china shop."

"You let bulls go into china shops here?" What in the world was he talking about?

"Never mind." Michael glanced at his watch and sighed. "Unfortunately, Elliot, I need to get home. I'm sorry."

He needed to get going because *Roxy* was at home.

No, scratch that.

He needed to get going because he needed to pick up Chloe. But after he picked up Chloe, I was certain he and Roxy were going to talk more. Get to know each other more. And who knew what else.

But I wasn't jealous.

Except I was. But why? I asked myself. I wanted the best for Michael and Chloe.

But that didn't change the fact that I disliked everything that was happening. And just because I felt one way didn't mean I had to act on it. That was the beautiful part of life.

Because you know who acted on impulses? Serial killers.

Not heartbroken women.

Do the right thing, even if it feels wrong. My dad always said that our emotions couldn't determine our virtues. Morals were definite; emotions were not.

Now that I knew he'd been a spy, that made even more sense.

"I understand," I finally said, my voice sounding a little too strained for my comfort. "Why don't you drop me at the office, and I'll call this Lindsay lady to confirm her alibi. Then I probably need to get home for the night anyway. I've been gone a lot lately."

The look Michael gave me made it clear he didn't really think I'd be heading home. I didn't want to think of myself as a workaholic, but maybe I was at times. Once I started on a project, I liked to complete it.

And when it came to something like a friend being missing, that only caused my resolve to strengthen.

"I'm sorry, Elliot." Michael glanced at me, an apology in his burdened gaze.

He didn't have to spell it out for me to know exactly what he was talking about. Roxy. His confusion. The disruption to this case.

"Take the time you need." I nearly had to force the words out. "You don't have to apologize."

Michael opened his mouth like he wanted to say more. But he didn't. Instead, we headed back to the office in silence.

When he pulled up in front of Driscoll and Associates, he leaned toward me for a moment. But, instead of kissing my cheek, he paused and swallowed hard.

"Let me know what you find out." His voice cracked again. "Please."

I nodded as I reached for the door, hating how quickly things had changed between us. "I will. I hope things go well tonight."

With that, I climbed from the minivan and went into the office.

As much as I loved being around Michael, it felt good to have a little space.

But I had to wonder if this was just the beginning and if a breathtaking chasm would soon exist between us.

CHAPTER EIGHTEEN

IT ONLY TOOK me twenty minutes to track down Lindsay and to confirm Beasley's alibi.

It looked like the arrogant coach could be cleared.

I frowned as I sat at my desk. It wasn't that I wanted the man to be guilty. I just wanted to find the Beltway Killer before he did something horrible to my friend. Throughout all of this, Velma's image was forefront in my mind. I had to keep it that way.

Michael and I had made some progress today, but we hadn't advanced enough to have any good leads on Velma yet. However, we couldn't give up hope. We *had* to keep looking. Maybe someone somewhere had seen something.

I rubbed my eyes before glancing at my watch. It was dinnertime, and my stomach rumbled to remind me that

I hadn't eaten much today. I knew that my mom would still be working and that my sister would probably be hanging out with her friends. That was our routine lately.

Instead of heading home, I went to my favorite place, The Board Room. Nothing sounded better right now than ordering a nice charcuterie board filled with fruit and cheese.

But when I walked into the place five minutes later, I spotted someone familiar sitting at my table.

And by my table, I meant the place where I always sat. The one in the corner where I could see everyone who came and went while also having a great view of the river outside.

Kitty Kight.

What was she doing here?

As soon as I saw her, she also spotted me and waved me over.

I hesitated.

Maybe I should pretend like I didn't see her and leave. That would be the easiest solution.

But it would also be cowardly, and I didn't want to be cowardly.

For that reason, I kept my chin up and started toward her. As soon as I reached the table, she pointed to the chair across from her. "Have a seat. Please. I could use some company."

Knowing her, there was a catch to this. There was

only one reason she would want me to sit with her right now. She wanted information.

"I'll be nice." She cast me a knowing look. "I promise. I'm not the shark that people make me out to be."

I stared at Kitty and then at the chair. Finally, I lowered myself across from her. Truthfully, I wanted to know what she knew. I wanted to know if she had any clues that Michael and I didn't have yet. If she did, that information might help us to find Velma sooner.

But I didn't want to do anything to put the investigation in jeopardy or to risk breaking the trust that Oscar and Michael felt with me right now.

I needed to proceed very carefully.

"I know you just think of me as a reporter, but the truth is we have a lot in common," Kitty started, closing her laptop screen and eyeing me from across the table.

"Do we?" I wasn't sure how Kitty knew that, considering we only talked twice before.

"Once I realized you worked for Driscoll and Associates, I did a little background on you. You grew up overseas, you're still single, you're in your late twenties, and you're intrinsically curious."

I pretended not to be impressed and continued to study her with a good dose of skepticism. "You grew up overseas?"

"I was a Navy brat. I wasn't *exactly* like you. But we lived in Okinawa, Guam, Puerto Rico, and even Germany for a while. It wasn't until I came back to the States for college that I settled down."

The woman sounded sincere. But she was a reporter. She was good at getting information from people by gaining their trust.

Maybe I should turn the tables and pry into her personal life a little more.

"How long have you lived in Storm River?" I asked her.

"Five years. It was the first place that hired me after I graduated from college. But I like it here. There's enough going on to keep my job interesting. Then again, newspaper work is a dying business. I'm not sure how much longer the *Storm River Daily* is going to be around. But I'll work for it for as long as I can."

"Sounds like you really love your job."

As soon as I said the words, the waitress appeared at our table with a charcuterie board full of fruit, cheese, and crackers.

Just what I'd been craving.

"Please, share this with me," Kitty said. "I always end up taking most of it home. But it's great food to snack on while I'm working."

Maybe I should have resisted, but my stomach grumbled and reminded me how hungry I was. For that reason, I grabbed a grape and popped it into my mouth.

"But, back to your statement—yes, I really do love my job," Kitty continued. "And this article about the Beltway Killer? It could be the story that makes my career. If the *Storm River Daily* ever does shut down, this could be my open door to a bigger newspaper. Maybe *The Washington Post*."

The woman certainly sounded driven. "How long have you been working on this Beltway Killer story?"

She made a cracker sandwich with some pepperoni and cheese. "From day one. I was there when that first victim disappeared. I've covered every disappearance since then."

"Good to know."

She grunted as she stared at me. "I saw you and Hunter talking."

"Hunter is a good cop." I meant the words. I couldn't say anything bad about the man.

Except that maybe he was the Beltway Killer.

I swallowed hard and tried to forget that theory. But, if I did that, would it end up being a huge mistake? Could it be a mistake that ended up getting me killed?

"So, have you discovered anything new?" Kitty bit into her cracker and stared at me.

"I thought we weren't going to talk about this," I reminded her, stabbing a strawberry with a toothpick.

"I'm just having conversation." Kitty stared at me, her eyes full of supposed innocence.

I'd be wise to be cautious. "It sounds to me like you're fishing for intelligence."

She made a face. "You mean information?"

"Maybe." Was that the correct saying? Either way, intelligence seemed a more fitting word right now. "I don't want to say anything that would compromise the investigation."

"Who said anything you tell me would do that?" Kitty stared at me.

I stared back. "Who says it wouldn't?"

A few seconds into our stare-off, Kitty chuckled and nodded. "I can appreciate someone who can be trusted with a secret. But I really do think that if we worked together, we'd find answers sooner."

Before I could say anything in response, a woman appeared at the table. At first, I thought she was our server, but it quickly became apparent that she wasn't.

The woman was probably in her mid-twenties, she wore plain jeans with a white top, and something about the creases surrounding her hazel eyes made her look distressed—or desperate. Maybe both.

"Are you that reporter?" the woman started, staring Kitty down.

Kitty tilted her head, a new look of caution in her gaze. "I am. And you are?"

"I've seen you around town investigating," the woman said. "And I need to talk to you."

"Why's that?" Kitty remained composed and professional.

The woman rubbed her throat, almost appearing like she didn't want to say whatever it was she'd come to say. "I think I was a victim of the Beltway Killer. I'm pretty sure I got away before he could kill me."

I sucked in a breath. Had I just heard her correctly?

Kitty and I exchanged a look.

I knew there was no way I was leaving right now—not until I heard this woman's story.

———

THE WOMAN—SHE said her name was Annabelle—sat down beside me. After I introduced myself, I ordered her a lemonade. She nibbled on a cracker, her gaze darting around, an obvious sign of her inner turmoil, as we waited for her drink to be delivered.

Kitty kept giving me a look, but she didn't ask me to leave.

So I stayed. And I would unless someone pointed me toward the door.

Actually, pointing wouldn't do the trick. Someone would have to push me there—and push me hard.

Kitty diverted her gaze back to Annabelle. "How did you find me?"

Annabelle shrugged, and her gaze skittered to the

window before she looked back at Kitty. "I heard you were writing about this story, so I looked you up. I've been trying to find a chance to talk to you."

"Have you gone to the police with your story?" I asked.

Annabelle seemed to withdraw into herself at the mention of the police. "No. I mean, the cops knew I disappeared and escaped. But I was a druggie at the time. They didn't take me very seriously. Sometimes, I can't blame them."

"Have you gone back to them since then with your suspicions?" Kitty lowered her voice, sounding more like a friend than a reporter. "Or maybe you could try a different officer."

Annabelle rubbed her hands across her sleeves, still looking ill at ease. "No. I don't like cops. I don't like talking to them. I don't like the way they doubt me. I can't go to them. The thought of it makes me want to puke."

Tension crossed Kitty's gaze, but she nodded. "I understand. To start, can any of this be on record?"

Annabelle shrugged. "I'd rather you hear my story first. Then we can decide. I question myself all the time. Wonder if I'm crazy. Sometimes, I don't feel like anyone will take me seriously."

"Fair enough." Kitty leaned back. "Why do you think you were abducted by the Beltway Killer?"

"Start from the beginning," I encouraged.

Kitty gave me a dirty look. I knew this was her meeting and that I just happened to be at the right place at the right time. But it was my friend who was missing. I didn't care what Kitty said—I had more at stake here.

Annabelle swallowed hard, and her eyes looked glazed. "When I was twenty-two, I worked as a waitress at this little dive bar near DC. I felt like someone was watching me from the shadows one night, but I didn't think much of it."

"Did you see this person's face?" Kitty asked.

Annabelle frowned. "No, I didn't. It was dark, and the band playing had a fog machine going. Anyway, when I got off work, I had a few drinks with some friends. I called an Uber when it was time for me to leave. But as I waited for it outside, this nice-looking car pulled up. A man was inside."

"What did he say?" Kitty asked.

"He said he'd noticed me in the bar and asked if he could give me a ride." Annabelle looked down at the table, her shoulders hunched. "I should have said no."

"What happened?" My heart pounded in my ears with anticipation—and dread. I knew the story was about to take a turn for the worse.

"I got inside." Annabelle's wavering gaze met mine. "And that's when my nightmare started."

CHAPTER NINETEEN

"I DON'T KNOW what I was thinking." Annabelle sniffled and drew in a shaky breath. "The man just sounded so nice. He drove an expensive car. I felt . . . lucky, I guess."

Kitty and I waited for her to gather herself before continuing. We were on the verge of something big. I could feel it in my bones.

"As soon as I closed the door, he used chloroform—at least, that's what I think it was—on me." Her voice broke as moisture filled her eyes. "When I woke up, I was at a house."

"A house?" I repeated, feeling another surge of hope. It was *something*. And I'd desperately been praying for that elusive something.

Annabelle rubbed her arms as if suddenly chilled.

"That's right. I was in a bedroom. The door locked from the outside, and it didn't even have a window. Everything had been removed except for a mattress and a blanket. I panicked when I woke up. Everything felt hazy. I'd had too much to drink. Thankfully, there was a bathroom connected to the space, so I could get some water."

"What happened next?" Kitty asked.

Annabelle shivered again. "He kept me in that room. He fed me. Made sure I was taken care of. He never even lifted a hand to me. It was . . . strange."

"Did he ever show you his face?" I asked.

"No, he wore a mask. Maybe I shouldn't say a mask. It was more like pantyhose that obscured his features. It was creepy."

Disappointment bit into me. "What about when you got in the car with him? Did you see him then?"

Annabelle shook her head. "He had a hat on, and he kept it low. His face was shadowed."

Kitty leaned closer. "Did the two of you ever talk? Did he say anything of note?"

"He did. He wanted to know about me. The way we interacted almost made me feel like he wanted to be my friend. It was so . . . strange."

"How did you get away?" I asked.

"I think I was there for almost two weeks. Every once in a while, he'd say something weird, like how he didn't really want to do this, but he had no choice. I begged him to let me go. But he said he couldn't. That what had to be done had to be done."

I sensed the emotions welling up in her, and I held back any more questions. She'd tell us the rest of her story in her time.

"He was acting more erratic, and I knew I had to escape if I wanted to stay alive," Annabelle continued. "I suspect he'd been putting some kind of drug in my food because I felt tired each time after I ate. I managed to pull a cover off an outlet. I broke it and used a sharp corner as a weapon. When he came in, I slashed it across his face. That gave me just enough time to run."

More hope surged in me. This could be the break we had been looking for, the information that led us to Velma.

"What next?" Kitty's voice barely contained her excitement.

"I ran and ran and ran. I must have tripped, though because I woke up in the woods. It was dark. I managed to go out to the road, but I passed out again. When I came to, I was in the hospital. Someone found me and picked me up."

Kitty shifted, almost appearing like she was on the edge of her seat. "Were the police called?"

She nodded, her lips trembling. "I told them my story. But they thought I was a drug addict. They didn't believe me—especially when heroin was found in my system and when there was no sign of abuse."

"You're telling me they didn't investigate at all?" I repeated, appalled at the notion.

"That's right. I mean, sure, the cop I talked to made it seem like he would verify what I'd told him. But he didn't. Once people have a certain impression of you . . . it's hard to be taken seriously."

"I'm sorry you were treated that way," I told her. "I'm glad you found us now."

Kitty gave me a look. I knew Annabelle hadn't sought me out, but it just seemed the simplest way to say things.

"Do you remember anything about the house or the area where you were held?" Kitty continued.

Annabelle shook her head, her arms trembling now. "I wish I did. But, like I said, he drugged me. My memories are all hazy."

"What about the area where you were picked up?" Kitty leaned forward. "Do you remember where it is? Anything that might give us an idea of where you were being held?"

"I can't remember." Annabelle shrugged, her eyes filling with moisture. "I know that's not helpful, and it's not what you want to hear. But it's the truth. The drugs did something to my mind, and I can't recall things that I should be able to recall."

"It's okay." I patted her hand. "You're doing great."

"I don't feel like I'm doing great. My life has been a mess ever since then. I can't seem to get myself back together."

"No one can blame you for that," I assured her. "It's a lot to process."

Annabelle pulled her gaze back up to meet mine. "I don't think that I was his first victim either."

Her words caused me to suck in a breath. What was she talking about?

This evidence, if it checked out, could turn this whole case upside down.

It looked like our first real clues had dropped into my lap—and I was eternally grateful to have been in the right place at the right time.

———

KITTY and I gave Annabelle a few minutes to drink some lemonade and eat a few bites of food. I was personally afraid that the woman might go into shock. Annabelle's motions seemed so frantic and jerky, as did her gaze.

I could only imagine the mental toll this was all having on her right now.

After a few more minutes, when Annabelle's glass was almost empty, we continued.

"Why do you think there were other victims?" I started, anxious to hear why she thought that.

"It was almost like this guy was working himself up to do this." Annabelle shook her head. "It's hard to describe, but he was nervous. The way he talked made him seem erratic. One minute, he'd be kind and seem like a friend. The next minute, it almost seemed like something snapped in him, like he needed to prove something."

"But did he say anything specifically that gave you the impression there were others before you?" I asked, craving more clarity.

"Again, it was just the way he talked. He kept saying things like . . . he wanted to see this through to completion. He needed to prove he could do this this time. It made me think that maybe there were other girls that got away."

"Did he say anything about any of them?" Kitty asked.

"I thought I heard him saying a name one time. Kiki, I think. I wish I could help you more."

"You're doing great," I reassured her. "Is there anything else about the place that you can remember? Was it on the water?"

She shook her head. "Like I said, I was locked in that room with no windows. When I escaped, I was so drugged that I don't remember much."

"What about sounds?" I continued. "Did you hear anybody else in the house? Or a train? Or even something simple like tree branches scratching the roof?"

She was silent for a moment, and I waited for her to

tell me that she didn't know anything else. Instead, she nodded slowly. "This is probably going to sound crazy."

"You can tell us anything," I told her. "It's okay."

She rubbed her thumbs together so hard that I thought she might start bleeding. Finally, she looked up again. "A couple times I thought I heard . . . a helicopter."

"A helicopter?" I repeated, keeping my voice even.

"I went on a helicopter ride once when I was a kid, and I remember that familiar *whoop whoop* sound that it makes. I kept thinking that's what I'd heard. But I don't know why I'd hear a helicopter. It doesn't make sense."

"So maybe you were close to a hospital or a news station. Maybe even a military base." I glanced over at Kitty, waiting for her confirmation.

But instead of seeing confirmation, I noticed her face looked pale.

"Kitty?" I repeated.

Kitty seemed to snap out of her stupor. She shook her head as her gaze came back into focus. "Sorry. That's . . . interesting."

But I could tell there was more to it. The new lead Annabelle had shared with us had triggered something in Kitty.

The question was, what?

CHAPTER TWENTY

I LEVELED my gaze with Annabelle, trying to keep my voice soft but firm. "I know this has been hard on you, but we need to call the police. They need to know what you just told us."

"I'm not sure that's a good idea," Kitty said from across the table.

I jerked my head toward her so fast that my neck ached. "What are you talking about?"

Certainly, Kitty wasn't so eager to get the lead on this story that she would compromise the investigation. Right? What other reason could she possibly have for saying that?

Kitty patted her hands in the air, as if encouraging my thoughts to slow down. "I'm just saying maybe we need to verify a few things first."

"You don't believe me?" Annabelle's hand flew across the table, knocking over her glass.

The remaining ice and lemonade inside spilled all over the wooden surface of the charcuterie board. I grabbed a napkin and quickly soaked up the liquid as Kitty began grabbing the melting cubes.

Annabelle hardly seemed to notice what she'd done. Instead, she stared at Kitty.

"It's not that I don't believe you." Kitty plucked the last piece of ice from the table. "I'm just saying that we should be careful here."

Annabelle shook her head, her nostrils flaring as offense set in. "You're just like everybody else. You think that, just because I have a past, I'm making this up."

"I'm not saying that," Kitty insisted, wiping her hand on a clean napkin. "I'm just saying that we need to check things out first."

I stared at Kitty, still perplexed at her reaction. It didn't fit my assumptions about the woman. "What's really going on?"

She shrugged, but the motion was so quick that it wasn't believable. "Nothing. Why?"

"You're acting strangely. You're not thinking rationally either."

Kitty's eyes narrowed. "Annabelle came to talk to *me* not *you*. I don't know why you're acting like you're in charge right now."

Maybe I deserved that. Maybe I didn't. I wasn't sure.

All of that seemed inconsequential right now.

Something was up. I stared at Kitty in a silent standoff.

Annabelle cleared her throat. "I did come to talk to you, Kitty. But I'm wondering if what Elliot said is right. I've kept this to myself for so long. Now someone else is missing."

Kitty didn't say anything for a moment.

Before anyone could try to talk me out of it, I pulled out my phone and put it to my ear. "I'm calling Hunter."

"Elliot . . ." Kitty started to reach for me, but I jerked away.

"I don't know why you're making a big deal of this." I tried to keep my voice down.

Before she explained herself, Hunter answered. I told him what we'd learned, and he promised to be at The Board Room ASAP.

But as I ended the call, I felt Kitty's red-hot gaze burning a hole through me.

I had no idea what was going on, but Kitty suddenly didn't seem quite as trustworthy as she had earlier. She was hiding something . . . but what?

AS ANNABELLE and Hunter talked at another table across the restaurant, Kitty and I gave them some space.

Hunter wanted a few minutes alone with Annabelle to hear her story. That was just as well because I wanted a few minutes alone with Kitty.

As we sat at the table, I turned to Kitty, unable to hold back my irritation. "What was that about?"

Kitty stared back, a touch of defiance in her gaze. "I don't know what you're talking about."

"Why in the world wouldn't you want Annabelle to talk to the police about this? This could be the break that helps them find a killer, that helps to keep innocent women safe."

She shrugged, still appearing nonchalant and defiant. "I'm just saying that maybe it would have been wise for us to look into things first."

"Maybe. Or we could be wasting valuable time. Time that could be used to find Velma." I continued to study Kitty, trying to figure out some kind of clue as to why she might be reacting like this. What had Annabelle said that had set her off?

Or maybe it hadn't been Annabelle. Maybe it had been what I'd said. I'd mentioned a hospital, a news station, or a military base. Had that triggered something in Kitty's mind?

It was apparent that Kitty wasn't going to give me that

answer. I supposed I was just going to have to wait or figure it out on my own.

Finally, twenty minutes later, Hunter motioned for Kitty and me to join him and we walked toward the table. I, for one, was anxious to hear Hunter's thoughts on this.

"You did the right thing by calling me," he said. "Thank you."

At least *one* person agreed with me. "What's next?"

Hunter let out a subtle breath, glanced at Annabelle, and then glanced back at me. "I'm going to look into the hospital records from that night Annabelle was admitted and see if I can find out who brought her in. If this man can remember the location where she was found, maybe that will give us a clue as to where she was being held."

"From what she told you, does this kidnapper's MO seem to match the MO of the Beltway Killer?" I held my breath as I waited for his answer.

"I can't say," Hunter said. "But it's a good possibility."

"You can never say much, can you?" Kitty practically rolled her eyes.

What was going on with her? Was she always this abrasive?

Hunter's gaze darkened. "Around you? No, I can't. Anything I say can and will be used against me, as the expression goes."

My eyes widened. The two of them had obviously

interacted before. There was apparently a history between them.

Hunter started to take a step toward the door, but he paused and observed Kitty a moment instead. "Say, isn't your brother a helicopter pilot? He works for the hospital, right? As a paramedic?"

Kitty's face went pale again. "That doesn't mean anything."

Suddenly, her reaction made sense. Kitty had heard about the helicopter and had known that Hunter might put two and two together.

But there had to be more to this than what I saw on the surface.

"How's your brother doing lately?" Hunter continued to study Kitty, an almost challenging look in his gaze.

Kitty crossed her arms and raised her chin. "He's doing just fine, thank you. If you want to know anything else, then you're going to need to talk to him yourself."

"Maybe I'll do that." Hunter offered a nod before departing the restaurant. When he did, I turned back toward Kitty and gave her a questioning glance. I was obviously in the dark, and she didn't owe me any explanation. But I sure would appreciate one right now.

She let out a long, drawn-out sigh before saying, "Yes, my brother was a pilot. But after he had shoulder surgery several years ago, he got addicted to opioids and found himself in a bad spot. He lost his job, his girlfriend, his house. But that doesn't mean he's a killer."

I heard the loyalty in her voice and tried to proceed carefully. "Does he live in this area still?"

She nodded. "Yes, he has for the past six years. But like I said, that doesn't mean anything."

Maybe it didn't. But I kept that information in the back of my mind.

Because, if what Annabelle said was true, then the Beltway Killer had actually begun his killing spree five years ago.

Which would have been a year after Kitty's brother had moved here.

Which made him a very viable suspect.

CHAPTER TWENTY-ONE

WHEN I WALKED into my house after leaving Kitty and Annabelle at The Board Room, I could tell my mother was still irked at me. Her motions were stiffer than usual, her smile nonexistent, and she gave off an overall irritated vibe.

I knew there was nothing I could tell her that would make things between us any better. Her mind was made up—I was in the wrong line of work, and I shouldn't have anything to do with trying to find Velma.

Instead of arguing with her, I said a quick hello and good night and then disappeared into my room, hoping for a few minutes by myself. But, a few minutes after I'd settled on my bed, someone knocked at my door.

I braced myself, trying to prepare for another argument with my mom.

Instead, Ruth walked in.

She shut the door behind her and sat on the end of my bed, pulling a leg beneath her. Her gaze searched mine, her normal teenage histrionics absent. "You and Mom still fighting?"

"I believe that Mama and I have reached what's often referred to as an impasse," I said. "Neither of us are going to budge on our feelings on the matter."

Ruth studied me a moment, her normally mischievous expression gone. "You're really trying to find a serial killer?"

"I'm just trying to find my friend."

Ruth started to say something, but a coughing fit stopped her. Her entire body bent forward as a filmy sound filled the air. Her face scrunched as if she were in pain.

I waited, knowing there was nothing I could do.

When Ruth finally was able to get a breath, she glanced up at me again. "Maybe you should cut Mom some slack and listen to her."

I couldn't believe I'd heard those words come from my sister's mouth, of all people. She was the one with the rebellious streak. If anyone supported my decision, I'd expected it to be Ruth.

I raised my chin, determined not to back down on my resolve. "Sometimes, you have to do what's right, even if it costs you everything. I can't live with myself if something happens to Velma."

"But how are Mom and I supposed to live with ourselves if something happens to you?"

I sucked in a breath. Ruth was right. This was hard on all of us, and, for every action that we took, there would be equal and opposite reactions. Consequences. That was how life worked.

That said, I knew I still couldn't back off on things. I only wished happy mediums were easier to find.

Another coughing fit seized her. My heart pounded into my ears as I realized just how bad Ruth's condition had become.

I'd known she wasn't doing well. I knew that she needed that lung transplant. But, looking at her now, I realized with absolute certainty that time was running out.

She needed that surgery, and she needed it soon.

"I'm going to go lie down." Ruth rose from the bed, her voice breaking and strained—probably from the trauma her coughing fit had put on her throat and vocal cords.

As she walked away, my heart ached with grief over my sister's situation. Ached with guilt as I felt myself being pulled in two different directions.

I had to figure out exactly what I was going to do.

But I knew right now that I wouldn't be able to sleep. Instead, I was going to look at all the papers I'd put together about these crime scenes. That seemed safe enough.

And like the perfect distraction from all my other problems.

Possibly even more effective than rhyming.

SITTING IN MY BED, I stared at the notebook on my lap where I'd been jotting down ideas for the past few hours.

Everything was quiet in the house. My mom and sister had obviously gone to bed a couple of hours ago. I'd sneaked out of my bedroom just long enough to grab some water and an apple before returning and closing my door.

As I stared at my notes, one thing bothered me . . . the locations where the victims had been left. There just didn't seem to be any rhyme or reason to the areas.

But I had a feeling their locations weren't random.

The first victim was left at the cemetery on top of Edna Murphy's grave. The second victim was left on top of Kenneth Jenkins' grave. Kate Snelling, the third victim and Hunter's fiancée, had been found on a trail at a state park. The fourth victim had been found at a lesser known presidential monument in a town square. And the fifth victim had been left at what locals in Storm River called the Matrix.

How were all those places linked?

Out of curiosity, I pulled out my computer and did some research on Edna Murphy, who'd lived from 1917 to 1991.

After jotting down a few details about her, I moved on to Kenneth Jenkins, who'd lived from 1964 to 2004. They definitely hadn't been in the same age group, nor did they appear to be related.

Edna had been a receptionist, and Kenneth had been a mechanic. They were from different parts of town, and I couldn't find anyone who connected them. I supposed I could talk to the victim's families and see if any information they shared might reveal something.

But I had a feeling it wasn't about a connection between the victims.

As I stared at the information, I sucked in a breath.

Kenneth Jenkins had lived at 1991 Samuel Adams Drive.

Edna Moore had died in 1991.

Was that just a coincidence? I didn't know, but it was worth exploring.

I looked at another piece of paper where I'd jotted down some notes, feeling like answers were close.

Kate Snelling had been found at the Samuel Adams Park on the presidential trail.

The fourth victim had been found at a presidential monument.

My pulse spiking, I did some quick research. Locals called the town square where the monument was located The Matrix. The final victim had been found at The Matrix overlook in Storm River.

Could it be that the killer was leaving clues as to where he would leave his next victim at every crime scene?

My heart rate continued to quicken.

I was pretty sure I was onto something.

I glanced at my watch. It was two a.m. I wasn't sure I had enough solid evidence to justify waking anybody up, nor was I sure this would actually help us to find the killer. But maybe it would just help us to get in his mind a little bit more.

I would wait until the morning before I told anybody. Maybe sleeping on it would bring additional clarity.

Until then, I stared at everything else I knew, reviewing the facts of the case.

The killer was most likely in his late twenties to early thirties. He had dark hair, was fit, and was on the taller side. If my assumptions were correct, this was a man who could blend in.

Based on what Annabelle had told me, he drove a nice car. He also may, in some way, be associated with helicopters. He either owned one, was a pilot, or lived close to a place utilizing the aircraft. She'd also made it sound like he'd come across as trustworthy.

When I put all of that together, whom did I have?

Was Kitty Kight's brother really someone I needed to look into? That was a definite yes.

What about Hunter? When I put aside my own biases, could he really be a suspect we needed to look at?

I didn't know. I didn't want to think so, but I had to be smart here.

The one thing I did know was that we were getting closer to answers.

And the closer to the answers we got, the closer we came to finding Velma.

CHAPTER TWENTY-TWO

THE NEXT MORNING, I desperately wanted to talk to Michael and run all my thoughts, theories, and updates past him.

I *could* wait until we both got into the office.

Or I *could* call him before work. I knew he'd be awake because he had to get Chloe ready for school.

That was why it didn't make sense when I found myself driving past his house instead.

Could it be because I was curious as to whether or not Roxy had stayed there last night? Was that the underlying reason, and I was using my semi-urgent updates as an excuse?

I didn't want to think of myself as the jealous type, but maybe I was dealing with that emotion more than I thought. Or maybe I was just curious.

Curiosity didn't sound as bad as jealousy, so I was going to go with that term. I had a healthy curiosity about Roxy, as well as the pressing urge to share my discoveries with Michael. It made sense to me.

As I headed down the road, I thought about what Michael had told me. Thought about Roxy's inoperable brain tumor. That she only had a few months to live and that all she wanted was to spend time with Chloe.

She had a sad story, that was for sure. And, if she was dying, Chloe deserved to be around her mom while they still had time together.

I wasn't sure where that left me. But I felt selfish to want to include myself in that mix.

Maybe I shouldn't feel selfish. Maybe I should be pushier. I'd never been in a situation like this before, however, and I wasn't sure what the right answer was.

All I was left with was my instincts. I wished I could refine them as easily as I could cull one of my Excel sheets. Life didn't work like that, however.

I slowed as I approached the driveway of Michael's house. Before I could even turn, I spotted Roxy stepping out of Michael's front door. He walked beside her toward her vehicle.

I pressed on my brakes, deciding at the last minute not to pull in. I didn't want to interrupt anything, and pulling up now would seem as awkward as a zebra joining a herd of horses.

But I watched as Roxy leaned against her car. Michael stood in front of her. Too close?

I wasn't sure.

Chloe stood on the porch, waving.

A moment later, Roxy was inside her car, Michael had closed her door, and Roxy backed out of her space.

As Roxy started down the long, narrow driveway, I continued forward. I wasn't sure what I was thinking, but, at the last minute, I pulled off onto the side of the road, just out of sight—I hoped.

And then I waited.

I hadn't planned on doing any of this. But my original plan had been a bad one. And, if that had been a bad plan, then this current decision was a *really* bad plan.

All my mental chiding didn't deter me from what I was about to do. I'd already silently committed.

When I saw Roxy's car pass, I waited a few seconds.

Then I pulled out behind her.

Where exactly was she going? Michael had mentioned something about some treatments she needed. But she apparently knew no one else in this area and had nowhere else she could stay—hence the reason she was at Michael's.

My curiosity grew.

I wasn't sure how long I'd follow behind her, but I decided I was going to do just that for a few minutes at least.

I stayed a decent distance behind Roxy so she wouldn't notice me. Michael had taught me that trick on tailing people. You should never get too close.

She cruised toward Storm River, drove through the town, and kept going until she finally stopped in front of a house on the outskirts of the area. She pulled into a circular driveway, climbed out, and bounded toward the front door. As she did, she looked like the picture of health.

That didn't mean she didn't have an underlying disease, I reminded myself. But that didn't mean she did either.

I strained my neck, trying to see who answered. But the person at the front door remained in the shadows and out of sight.

Something about this whole situation didn't sit right with me. Maybe I would stay here until I figured out exactly who Roxy was talking to and why.

For Michael's sake.

For *Chloe's* sake.

I parked across the street and waited. I hoped I didn't get caught because I didn't know how I would explain myself if I did.

But something raised all kinds of warning bells in my mind.

I glanced at my watch. I needed to be at work in less

than an hour. Finding Velma was more important than figuring out what Roxy might be up to, I supposed.

But finding out what Roxy might be up to was still important.

Especially since people I cared about were involved.

———

THIRTY MINUTES LATER, Roxy still hadn't left the house. I'd jotted down the address and taken a quick picture. Then I knew I needed to get into work. At this rate, I could stay here all day and still not figure out what was going on.

Besides, I didn't want to be late getting into the office. I had a lot to talk about with Oscar and Michael.

When I stepped inside, I spotted Michael standing near his desk.

Guilt blasted through me.

Should I tell him what I'd done? How exactly would I bring up the fact that I followed Roxy without sounding psycho? There was a good possibility that I couldn't.

Maybe I should have thought that through earlier.

"Elliot!" Oscar bellowed. "In my office. Now. Michael, you too."

Like obedient children, we walked into his space and sat down across from him. He propped his legs up on his desk and popped some pistachios into his mouth. But something about his actions didn't look as casual as usual. It was almost like he was going through the motions, trying to look more laid-back than he was.

"What's new?" he asked. "Did either of you discover anything since we last spoke?"

"I wish I could say I did," Michael started. "Unfortunately, I wasn't able to do much research last night. I'm sorry."

I wondered exactly what he *had* done last night that had prevented him from doing any more work. Was it just spending time with Chloe? Or had some new development happened with Roxy?

I pushed down the surge of insecurity that I felt.

No, curiosity. I needed to keep telling myself that was what that emotion was.

"Elliot? How about you?" Oscar turned his beady gaze on me.

"As a matter of fact, I did make some headway." I sucked in a deep breath before launching into my meeting with Annabelle and Kitty.

"I'm kind of surprised you didn't call us last night and tell us what you learned." Michael studied me for a minute, an unreadable look in his gaze.

I shrugged, trying to pull myself together. "It was kind of late. I knew there wouldn't be much we could do last night."

"Maybe you're right." Michael leaned back in his seat,

a far-off look in his eyes. "But at least this gives us something to go on. There could have been other victims who were just never identified."

"That would explain how this guy executes his crimes so perfectly," Oscar said. "I've always thought that was strange how he left no evidence behind. Maybe it's because he practiced first."

I shivered at his stark words. But they could very well be true. This guy could have a long history that we didn't know about. That would explain a lot.

"And the helicopter?" Michael added. "That's strange."

I licked my lips, feeling like I was throwing a friend in front of a herd of stampeding cattle. But I would be doing a disservice to this investigation if I didn't share everything. "It turns out that Kitty Kight's brother pilots helicopters, and he also has a history of drug addiction."

Oscar stared at me. "So you're thinking he could be our guy?"

I shrugged. "I don't know. But maybe he's somebody worth looking into. Plus, as soon as Kitty heard the word *helicopter*, she turned pale. Was it because she's afraid we'd assume it was her brother? Or was it because she thinks it could be her brother?"

"Good points," Michael said. "We should definitely look into him."

"There's one other thing." I reached into my bag and

pulled out the papers I'd printed out detailing all the information that I had uncovered last night. "I may be way off base here, but I think I found the connection between the secondary crime scenes—the areas where the bodies were left."

I handed them both identical sheets of paper. I'd even placed arrows on my flow charts so I could show the connections between each of the locations and victims.

I knew Oscar and Michael were capable of reading what I'd written, but I talked it out anyway. When I finished, I held my breath, waiting for their reactions.

I hoped they wouldn't think I was crazy.

Because I really thought I could be onto something.

"Good work, Elliot." Oscar nodded slowly, something close to admiration in his gaze. "You just might have a future in this business after all."

Was this the first time he'd ever thought that? It didn't matter. I'd take the compliment.

"I agree," Michael said. "Good job. I'm not sure if this will help lead us to the killer, but it's good information. It gives us additional insight into this killer. He's definitely smart. Sneaky. And, if you're right, it's almost like he's playing a game with us and trying to prove he's superior."

I found myself beaming at their kind words. "Thank you."

"Why don't the two of you go talk to Kitty Kight's brother?" Oscar said. "I'm going to study these crime-scene photos again. I'll also make a call to one of my police contacts and see if I can get any information from him about which hospital Annabelle was taken to that night."

I stood and nodded, relieved that we seemed to be making some progress. "That sounds good."

A few minutes later, Michael and I left Oscar's office, grabbed our things, and stepped outside.

I thought I might feel a touch of relief being out from under Oscar's watchful gaze. But I didn't. I still felt tense.

I knew it was, in part, because of what I'd seen this morning, and in part because I didn't know where Michael and I stood right now.

But we were about to spend the whole day together, so I was probably about to find out.

CHAPTER TWENTY-THREE

"YOU'RE DOING GOOD WORK, ELLIOT," Michael said as we climbed into his minivan. "It's hard to believe I only started training you a little more than a month ago. You've picked up things quickly."

"Thank you. Right now, I really want to find Velma more than anything." I pulled my seatbelt on.

"Me too." He glanced at me and hesitated a moment. He opened his mouth like he wanted to say something then shut it again. A moment later, he said, "We need to figure out where Kitty Kight's brother lives."

"Yes, we do." Talking to him would be the perfect distraction from all my other problems.

I pulled out my phone and typed in Kitty's name. On her social media page, she'd listed her family members.

There was only one brother listed, so I clicked on his name.

Kyle Kight.

A few minutes later, we had his address, and we were on our way. Kyle lived about thirty minutes from where we were, so Michael and I would have the whole ride to talk. I wasn't sure if I dreaded that or felt excited.

After a few minutes of silence fell, I knew I had to initiate some conversation. I cleared my throat before asking, "So what's new?"

Michael shrugged and rubbed his jaw. "I don't know."

I wasn't used to hearing him sound so uncertain. Michael was the confident one, the guy who knew what he wanted, who never doubted his next move.

So something was definitely wrong.

I needed to ask more questions, even if I wasn't sure I wanted to hear the answers. "How's Roxy?"

"She was over at my place again last night. Just to be with Chloe," he quickly added. "Her head was hurting, and she was obviously in pain but trying not to show it. I don't think Chloe noticed."

"I'm sorry to hear that." I meant the words. I didn't like hearing about anybody being in pain.

Michael frowned. "Me too."

"Is Roxy staying at your place until you get home?"

"She had to go to the hospital for a treatment this

morning," Michael said. "I offered to go with her, but she wanted to go alone."

My heart thrummed in my ears. Roxy hadn't been telling him the truth—that was why she wanted to go alone.

I nibbled on my lip.

Maybe I should give the woman the benefit of the doubt. Maybe she'd stopped at this other house on the way to treatment. But I seriously doubted that.

Something was fishy about her story.

"Does she know anybody else in town?" I finally asked. "Maybe they could go with her sometime."

Michael shook his head. "No, Roxy's not from around here. Besides, if she knew anybody else in town, she could stay with them instead of me."

I swallowed hard but the lump in my throat remained. "I see. I'm surprised she lined up treatment here instead of wherever she was living."

"Me too. She said she did it to be close to Chloe. That's sweet . . . I guess."

"What about her family? Can't they help her?"

"They disowned her. Apparently, she burned too many bridges. Sometimes, I just want to burn the bridge too. Then I remember all the people who forgave me and offered a second chance after I screwed up. How can I not afford someone else that same grace?"

I couldn't argue with that.

Was this my cue to fess up?

I opened my mouth, but the words wouldn't leave my lips. How did I explain I'd followed Roxy? What would Michael think of me once he learned what I'd done?

I didn't know.

But I felt certain that Roxy wasn't telling the truth. What I couldn't figure out was why. *Why* wasn't she being forthcoming? How could she possibly benefit from lying to Michael about this disease?

Even more than that, should I let Michael discover it for himself? Would he resent me if I told him? Or would he resent me if I didn't tell him?

I had so many questions, and so little answers.

"Does Chloe still enjoy spending time with her?" It seemed like a safe enough question. But part of me didn't want to know. I didn't want to think about Chloe getting close only to get hurt.

"She seems to. Like I said, Chloe always liked to talk about her mom. She keeps saying this is an answer to prayer. But she did ask about you yesterday." Michael cast a quick glance my way.

My heart lifted. "Did she?"

"She did. She wanted to invite you over for dinner with us. I told her you had other things to do."

"Of course." I couldn't help but feel a bit disappointed. Was that the real reason why Michael hadn't invited me over—because he'd assumed I was busy? Or was it because he wanted more alone time with Roxy?

There were so many things that left me uncertain.

I changed the subject. "So, have you talked to Grayson lately?"

I was hoping his friend might have an update for us about the whole situation with the jump drive. But, deep inside, I knew the truth was that the jump drive was gone. I might not ever know what information had been stored on the device.

"Grayson did call yesterday, but he didn't have any updates. I'm sorry. I've been sidetracked, but I haven't forgotten about your father's death and finding answers for you."

"The good news is I haven't noticed anyone following me or watching me this week." My words sounded placating.

"That's one way to look on the bright side, I suppose."

Before we could say anything else, we pulled up to an apartment complex.

It looked like we were here.

At Kyle Kight's place.

I only hoped he might have some answers for us.

"I ALREADY TALKED to my sister, I already talked with the police, and I ain't got anything else to say to you."

Kyle Kight was a charmer, that was for sure.

The man reminded me of Kitty, only a larger, more foul-mouthed version. Where Kitty was small and athletic, Kyle was tall and heavyset. He wasn't necessarily overweight, but he had big bones and shoulders. Just like Kitty, he had a smattering of freckles across his face and wheat-colored curls atop his head.

For someone who wasn't that much older than I, he looked like he'd already lived a lot of life.

We stood outside his door, and he remained inside. The look in his eyes just dared us to invite ourselves in.

He definitely wasn't the hospitable type.

Instead, I was perfectly content to remain where I was, Michael by my side. Besides, the inside of Kyle's apartment looked like, as my mother would say, a pigpen. Trash appeared to litter every visible surface, dirty clothes were strewn on the floor, and even the smell—a mix of dirty laundry and rotting food—made my stomach turn.

"We heard that you were a helicopter pilot," I started.

Kyle crossed his bulky arms. "That's right."

"Maybe you could tell us where someone might have heard a helicopter coming and going." I decided to try a different approach than the one I'd originally intended using.

"It's like I told my sister, it could be a number of places." He practically grunted as he said the words. "Sure, there are hospitals and news stations and military bases. However, if someone heard a helicopter coming and going from a property, it was most likely a private helicopter."

"People have those?" I shouldn't be surprised. I really shouldn't.

I just couldn't imagine living that kind of life. I'd be happy just to have a reliable car that was painted all one color.

Kyle nodded. "Oh, yeah. People definitely have those. Especially people around here. All these important locals want to get to work as quickly as they can, so many of them have their own helicopters that they take right from their house to their job. Then they scream about protecting the environment, like they're the ones battling it on the front lines. Hypocrites."

"Where do they land once they get to their job?" I tried to picture it but couldn't.

"Usually? On top of buildings. We're talking about very wealthy people who have their own choppers and most have their own businesses. It's a nice setup for some of these people."

"So the Beltway Killer might be wealthy." I added that information to my mental checklist. "Is there a way to track who has a helicopter in this area?"

Kyle shrugged, seeming to loosen up just a bit. "They would have to have a license. I'm sure if you contacted the Federal Aviation Association, they'd have a list of everyone who has a license in the area—if they'd give you that information. However, just because a person has a helicopter doesn't mean they have a license. A lot of times people hire pilots for them."

"And if someone wanted to go about hiring a pilot, where would they do that?" Michael asked.

"There are websites you can check that will list pilots for hire. But it's going to be a big task trying to track down just who hired who." Kyle paused and eyed me. "You're not going to ask if it was me?"

"Was it you?" I said.

"It wasn't. Besides, when one of the women disappeared, I was locked up. You can check it out for yourself."

I would be doing just that.

But I had to admit that Kyle Kight didn't fit my profile. He wasn't suave, he wasn't wealthy, and, based on his sloppy apartment, he wasn't organized enough to pull off these murders.

CHAPTER TWENTY-FOUR

BACK IN THE MINIVAN, Michael let out a breath, looking as exhausted as I felt. I knew my reason—I'd stayed up all night, determined to do whatever I could to find Velma.

Was he exhausted from worrying about Velma also? Or was it because of Roxy? Perhaps it was a combination of the two.

"It looks like we have some work ahead of us," he muttered.

"Yes, we do." I frowned. Kyle had been our best lead, and now we needed a new one.

Finding out everyone who owned a helicopter in this area was going to be time-consuming, and the last thing I wanted to do was sit behind a computer. Time wasn't on our side right now, and I couldn't forget that fact.

"Can you go through what Annabelle told you again?" Michael turned toward me, making no effort to drive. At least the AC was already coming through the vents, helping to ward away some of the day's stifling warmth.

"Sure." I recounted what Annabelle had said to Kitty and me last night at The Board Room.

"Wait . . . she actually thought she heard a name?"

I thought I'd said that earlier, but maybe my lack of sleep was getting to me.

"That's right. It's sad to think that someone could have just disappeared, and no one really noticed."

"That's why this guy targets these women. He knows they're relatively alone."

It still pained me to think of Velma as being one of those people, especially since she had us. I should have done more for her.

"What name did she say?" Michael asked.

"Kiki or something."

I glanced at Michael again and saw the wheels were still churning in his mind. Had the name sparked something in him? The way his gaze flickered definitely made me think so.

"What are you thinking about?" I asked.

"It's probably nothing." He shrugged, but I could still tell he was bothered.

"Tell me anyway."

He let out a long breath and readjusted his baseball cap. "You remember that girl I told you about? The one I'd been dating, but Jono stole her from me?"

"I do."

"Her name was Krista, but everyone called her Kiki. It's kind of a unique name, you know?"

"Okay . . ." I still wasn't sure where Michael was going with this.

"I haven't heard from her in years."

I tried to fill in the blanks. "You think the Beltway Killer took her?"

Michael shrugged, took his hat off again, and ran a hand through his hair. "I know it sounds outlandish. Maybe it is. But it was like she disappeared off the face of the earth. I just thought she was flighty but . . ."

"Exes have a way of disappearing off our radars. Why don't you look her up? You'll probably find her on social media." His dilemma seemed like something that could be cleared up pretty easily.

"Maybe I'll do that, just to make myself feel better." He pulled out his phone and did a quick search before shaking his head. "There's nothing there."

"Nothing at all?" I'd honestly expected a quick resolution.

"Nothing at all," he confirmed.

"What about mutual friends?" I suggested. "Is there

anyone you could call who might have talked to her recently?"

"There are a couple of people ..."

"You should follow up, especially if it makes you feel better."

He stared at me, questions in his gaze. "You don't think I'm crazy?"

"Not at all. Worrying about a friend is never crazy."

With a grateful smile, Michael dialed a number. When he ended the call, he announced that his friend hadn't heard from Kiki either. I'd gathered that much from what I'd heard of the conversation.

"Maybe she just moved and left everyone behind," I suggested. "When was the last time you spoke?"

"Probably six years ago."

"The Beltway Killer didn't start killing until three years ago. If Annabelle's correct, then maybe five. There's no reason to think he went back that far."

"You're probably right." But Michael sounded unconvinced.

I studied his face another moment. "It's still bothering you."

"Yeah, for some reason, it is. Something's just not sitting right with me."

"There's only one thing I can think of you can do," I said.

He glanced at me, curiosity in his gaze. "What's that?"

"Call Jono. See if he's talked to her."

Michael's eyebrows shot up before sinking down again as the thought seemed to settle on him. "You might be right. If anyone's talked to her, it would be him."

I WATCHED as Michael punched something on his phone screen. I found it interesting that he still had Jono's number in his cell, but I didn't say anything. Michael had his reasons.

Instead, I listened to the one-sided conversation.

"Jono," Michael started. "It's Michael."

I couldn't hear what Jono said, but, based on Michael's scowl, he didn't appreciate whatever it was.

"Listen, you know I wouldn't call you unless it was urgent," Michael continued. "When was the last time you talked to Krista?" Michael's scowl grew deeper. "Yes, that Krista."

They said a few more things to each other until finally Michael ended the call and turned toward me. "He said he hasn't talked to Krista in six years or so."

My eyebrows shot up. "Six years, huh? Did he seem concerned?"

"Not really. But you know how Jono is. He thinks of one person. Himself."

Michael and Jono had been best friends until Krista

came between them. It was clear now that Michael didn't think highly of the man, for a multitude of reasons. That was probably why Michael had been so bothered when I'd gone on a couple of dates with Jono.

I'd only done so because I thought Jono might somehow be connected to my father's time here in the States. But it turned out to be a misunderstanding. Best I could tell, Jono had not interacted with my father—or even known him, for that matter.

"What else did he say?" I asked. "Anything?"

"Not really. He said I already seem to have enough women to juggle. Why did I want to add one more?" Michael scowled again.

"How does he know about Roxy?"

"I'm not sure. Word gets around town quickly about these kinds of things, though."

I could see that.

Michael sighed again. "I guess I could try a couple of Krista's other friends and see what they say."

"If it will help ease your thoughts, then why not?"

Michael glanced at his watch. "But we do need to get going. I don't want to waste time, especially since I can't put in any overtime at work right now."

"How about I drive while you make the phone calls?" I suggested.

Michael glanced at me. "Are you sure?"

"Of course."

Maybe driving would help keep me focused on something else other than the multitude of problems wrecking my life like a monsoon ravaging the jungle.

CHAPTER TWENTY-FIVE

I KEPT my hands on the steering wheel as I drove, half listening to the conversation Michael was having beside me. Oscar had called us and told us the general area where Annabelle had been found, and we were going to check it out.

Beside me, Michael's voice sounded friendly as he talked to various friends of Krista. But, from what I could gather, nobody had seen her recently. As in, within the past six years.

After his third call, Michael lowered his phone again.

"Anything?" I cast a quick glance his way.

"No. It's like she disappeared off the face of the earth —just as I feared."

"Did she tell anybody that she was leaving?"

Michael's jaw flexed before he shook his head and said, "That's the thing. Krista told people she was going to go to New York City. So when her friends stopped hearing from her, they just assumed she'd moved. But that was the last anybody saw or heard from her."

"What about her things? Did she pack everything up and take it with her? Where was she living at the time?"

"If I remember correctly, she was renting a room from a family. She basically only had a couple of suitcases there. The place was furnished otherwise."

"Do you know if she took those suitcases when she left?"

"That's a good question." Michael frowned. "It's something worth looking into. But I don't remember the name of the family she was renting the room from. I'll see if I can figure it out."

As he did that, we reached the area where Annabelle had apparently been found. It was an upscale area only a few minutes from DC. Don't get me wrong, Storm River was also upscale. But this was a different kind of upscale.

The large, sprawling homes were located at the end of long lanes down deep wooded lots. The roads were clean and freshly paved. We'd even passed a limo en route.

I tried to imagine Annabelle here. To imagine where she may have escaped from.

There were definitely no hospitals or military bases nearby.

Maybe what she'd heard had been a personal heli-copter as Kyle had suggested. It made the most sense.

In fact, maybe the house where Annabelle was being kept was one of these large ones. Each of the properties probably contained at least six acres. People could come and go easily without anyone knowing anything or without neighbors being able to hear any screams.

The thought wasn't comforting.

There was so much I still didn't know. So much that still didn't make sense.

"I found the name of the couple she was staying with." Michael looked up from his phone. "I just tried to call, but they didn't answer. We're about fifteen minutes away from their place. How do you feel about driving past?"

"I'm game if that's what we need to do." I still wasn't sure this was going to lead anywhere. It seemed like a bit of a stretch. But I knew that Michael needed to do this for his own sanity.

He spelled out some directions to me, and I took off toward Krista's old place. I hoped for Michael's sake that he was able to find some answers.

A FEW MINUTES LATER, Michael's phone rang again. To my surprise, I heard him say Jono's name.

Michael told him the update, mumbled a few more things, and then turned toward me after he ended the call.

"He wants to come with us," Michael announced.

I flinched. "Why would he want to do that?"

Jono had never shown any interest in our investigations before—nor had he particularly shown any concern for other people. He embodied the term "hedonistic."

"Apparently, the people Krista was staying with hate me, so Jono insists they won't open up to me about anything." Michael narrowed his eyes, as if that fact displeased him.

"Why would they hate you?" I had a hard time believing anyone could hate Michael. He was an all-around good guy.

"Because they think that I broke Kiki's heart." Michael's scowl deepened.

That didn't match what I knew about their breakup. "She was the one who cheated on you, right?"

"That's what happened, but apparently that's not what she told them."

"Why would she lie to them?"

"I'm not 100 percent sure. I know the man worked for Jono's dad but had been laid off at some point—and he was pretty angry about it. Maybe Kiki didn't want to add any more fuel to the fire, so to speak. There was already a lot of tension there."

Interesting logic. "So are we going to meet Jono?"

"He's not too far away right now," Michael said. "He's coming back from DC and said he would meet us at a rest stop so we could ride together."

I did a double take at Michael, trying to get his read on this situation. "And you're okay with this?"

He shrugged. "I'm not okay with any of this. But I'll do what I have to do to find answers."

It was his call. Sure, having both of them in the car seemed a little awkward. Throw in Hunter, and I could star in my own episode of *The Dating Game: Carpool Version*. Believe it or not, that had been a show in Yerba.

I could deal with this mashup if that's what I needed to do.

Several minutes later, I pulled into a rest area as Michael directed. Jono and his Bentley were already waiting there for us.

As soon as we pulled up beside him, Jono stepped out and smoothed the sleeve of his pale blue polo shirt. The man always looked like a million bucks. I supposed when a million bucks was worth about as much to you as a hundred bucks would be to a normal person, then there was nothing weird about that.

His face, however, looked grim as he approached us. "Thanks for letting me tag along."

Michael only grunted in response.

"I know it sounds weird, but I've been thinking about

Krista lately—since before you called me earlier. I wondered whatever happened to her. Now that you brought all of this up . . . I need to know that she's okay."

Had Jono actually cared about this woman? I didn't want to sound surprised, but I was. Jono wasn't the settling down, one-woman type of man. At least, that's not how he came across.

I offered a polite smile. "You're welcome to ride with us."

Jono glanced at me and then glanced at Michael's old minivan as if it was beneath him to ride in it.

If he thought this was bad, he should try my beat-up silver Buick with the red door. I was just thankful to have a car that ran. But I knew many people thought of cars as status symbols.

I knew *exactly* what my car said about me and my status.

That I was lowly and poor.

Quite honestly, I'd rather be poor and simple than rich and complicated. But I knew most people around here wouldn't understand my viewpoint. It wasn't the American way.

"Are you sure you don't want me to drive?" Jono nodded behind him at his vehicle.

"I'm sure." I put my foot down, knowing it was best if Michael and I stayed in control.

I waited for Jono's reaction, wondering if he'd scoff at the idea or change his mind.

After a moment, he shrugged and nodded. "Okay then. Let's get going."

CHAPTER TWENTY-SIX

"SO WHY ALL THE interest in Krista now?" Jono leaned toward the front seat.

"Something we learned recently made me think about Krista," Michael said, his voice even—not too friendly, not too cold. "You know me—I don't like to leave any stone unturned."

"There has to be more to it than that."

Michael rubbed his jaw, controlled tension radiating from him. "If you really want to know, some new evidence has come forward that suggests Kiki could have been a victim of the Beltway Killer."

Shock coursed through me that Michael had actually shared that much. But he must have a good reason for it. Maybe he knew Jono would be more likely to share if he knew that information.

Jono sucked in a breath. "I thought this sicko only had five victims so far."

"There could be more victims than the police suspect," I said quietly. "It makes sense when you think about it."

Jono didn't say anything for a moment before blurting, "How do you guys know all of this?"

"We can't tell you that." I didn't want to throw Annabelle under the bus. I thought Jono might be trustworthy, but I couldn't risk the wrong person getting their hands on that information. If word got out, Annabelle could be a target again.

Jono let out a grunt. "I hate to think about that. Krista was a nice girl. I've always imagined her up in New York working as a receptionist for some big company with a swanky building. I figured she was enjoying the social scene there."

"Let's hope that is the case." Michael's voice sounded grim as he said the words. "But I'd like to know for sure before I let this go."

"You guys are really serious, aren't you? You think the Beltway Killer could have snatched her." Jono shook his head. "This keeps getting worse and worse."

Neither Michael nor I said anything for a moment.

"What else have you discovered?" Jono asked, instantly acting like he was the newest member of our team. "Are you guys getting closer to finding this guy?"

"We don't know," Michael said. "But we're tracking down any evidence that we might find."

"Do you have any suspects yet?" Jono continued.

Michael glanced over his shoulder. "Since when have you cared about things like this?"

"I've been following this case for a long time," Jono said. "Everybody in the area has. Besides, maybe I like to think of myself as an armchair detective."

Michael let out another grunt. "I can't see that."

I could tell this was going to be a fun car ride. Thankfully, we were almost at Krista's old place.

A few minutes later, I pulled up to a moderately sized house in a little suburban neighborhood. An old, beat-up Ford truck sat in the driveway, indicating that someone was probably home.

I put the minivan into Park and turned to my passengers.

"Let's go see what we can find out," I said. "You two be on your best behavior or you're both walking home."

———

A MAN in his sixties with a thin build answered the door. He glanced at us in confusion for a moment before his gaze fell on Michael.

"Mr. Lawson," Michael started. "You may not remember me—"

His eyes narrowed. "I know who you are."

Michael let out a sigh before murmuring, "Michael Straley."

"You played for the Mets." A mix of admiration and disgust mingled in the man's voice. "It was a shame when you had to stop playing because of your knee."

"I think so too." Michael nodded in agreement.

When the man's gaze fell on Jono, a slight smile tugged at his lips. "And if it isn't Jono Harris. It's been a long time."

Jono extended his hand, and the two offered a hearty handshake. Jono's warm reception was vastly different than the cold shoulder the man had given Michael.

"Good to see you too, sir," Jono said. "This is our friend, Elliot."

The man nodded in acknowledgement before looking back at Michael and scowling. "What brings all of you by here?"

Michael nodded at Jono, indicating that he should take the lead. It seemed like a good call considering Mr. Lawson's reaction to Michael. Anyone who broke Kiki's heart was obviously not welcome here. Maybe it was a good thing the man didn't know the whole story. Even Jono wouldn't be welcome if that was the case.

"We've been trying to get in touch with Krista, and I wondered if maybe you'd heard from her?" Jono started.

"Can't say I have in probably . . . six years." He

shrugged. "It's too bad. My wife and I thought of Krista like a daughter, so it was a shock to both my wife and me when she didn't keep in contact after she left."

"She rented a room from you, correct?" I chirped in.

Mr. Lawson nodded. "That's right. The FROG. It's a three-car garage so the accommodation was ample and she even had her own bathroom. My wife and I have been renting that room out to college kids in the area ever since we moved here fifteen years ago. We couldn't have kids of our own, so it was fun to have some young blood in the house with us."

"We're hoping you can tell us a little bit about the last time you saw Krista," Jono said.

Mr. Lawson's eyes narrowed again, this time with concern. His hand went to his heart, and I wondered if he had some kind of condition. Now that I thought about it, he did look a little frail. If that was the case, we needed to tread carefully.

"What do you mean?" he asked. "Is everything okay?"

"Like we said, we haven't been able to get in touch with her, and as far as we know, this was the last location where she was seen," Jono said. "We just wondered about the circumstances surrounding her leaving."

The man shrugged. "She wanted to go to New York City. Told us that that's what she was going to do. She sent us a text when she was on her way, and that was that. Never heard from her again."

"So all of her stuff is gone?" Michael asked.

Mr. Lawson's gaze narrowed. "She didn't have much stuff. The apartment was furnished. But her clothes and toiletries were gone, if that's what you're asking."

"And I'm assuming her car was gone also?" I asked, trying to get the complete picture.

"That's right. There didn't seem to be anything suspicious about her departure. She was all paid up on her bills and she gave us two weeks' notice, so there were no hard feelings on our part."

"Have you rented out her place since then?" Michael asked.

Lawson shook his head. "As a matter of fact, we haven't. We were going to, but then my wife and I decided we should do some traveling. See more of the world. We decided to take a few years off from renting the space and, unfortunately, once we stopped, we never started again."

"Is there any chance we could see the apartment?" I asked.

Lawson tilted his head and rubbed his chest again. "Why do I have a feeling that there's more at stake here than what you're letting on?"

"We just want to make sure that she is okay." I stared at him, offering my most affable expression. "No one's heard from her since she left the area."

"I hope you're not accusing me of anything." As soon

as he said the words, a wall of defensiveness seemed to appear around him.

"Oh, no, sir," I rushed. "We're just trying to track her down, like we said."

After staring at us another moment as if trying to ascertain if we were trustworthy, Lawson finally nodded. "I certainly don't have anything to hide. Knock yourself out."

That was the second time I'd heard this weird American expression. I was starting to get used to the sayings, but I was far from understanding most of them.

Lawson led us inside through a well-decorated home and up the stairway at the other side. As we walked through, I glanced at the pictures of Mr. Lawson and the woman I assumed was his wife. Other pictures also graced a table behind the couch—pictures of whom I assumed were family members. I even saw a picture of Krista.

"Krista had a separate entrance near the garage that she usually used so she didn't have to intrude on our space," Lawson explained. "Not that we would have minded. Krista was a sweet girl. She didn't deserve to have her heart broken." He scowled at Michael.

Michael opened his mouth as if to refute the statement but then closed it again. It probably wasn't worth the effort to try to explain what had happened.

A moment later, the four of us stood in Krista's old

apartment. Like Lawson had said, the space was large and had everything she would have needed. The walls were beige, and the cabinets and trim were stained a light oak color.

"I'll give you a few minutes," Lawson said before disappearing back down the stairway.

As soon as he left, I turned to Jono. "How long had the two of you been broken up when she moved?"

He stared at the wall a moment before shrugging. "Probably four or five months, if I had to guess. Why?"

"Did she start dating anybody in the meantime?" I asked.

"Not that I know of."

"You ever talk to her again after that?" Michael asked, opening a drawer.

"We would call or text on occasion. But it wasn't very personal. She didn't share very many details about her life with me. Any more questions?"

"Not yet," I told him.

I wandered around the room, trying to tap into my overbearing sense of detail. Had Krista left anything here that might indicate what had happened to her?

I knew we most likely wouldn't find anything. It had been a long time since Krista lived here, and no doubt the room had been cleaned more than once. Still, I would be remiss if I didn't check and double-check everything.

I looked in the cabinets of the little kitchenette. In the fridge. Under the bed and behind curtains.

Finally, I paused by her nightstand. I opened the drawer and saw a Bible inside. The hardback cover made it look rather generic, like something that had been left at a hotel instead of a personal copy.

I almost slipped it right back into the drawer when I saw that a couple of the pages had folds in them. Out of curiosity, I opened the cover. On the inside was a set of notes that had been quickly scribbled in pencil.

It read, "helicopter rides." Beside it was a date going back six years ago.

I sucked in a breath.

Did this tie Krista with the Beltway Killer?

I didn't know. But my guess was yes.

CHAPTER TWENTY-SEVEN

"WHAT DOES a helicopter have to do with any of this?" Jono glanced back and forth between Michael and me as we stood in the apartment.

"Some new evidence has come to light indicating that the killer may in some way be associated with a helicopter," I said somewhat reluctantly.

Jono stared at us, still looking perplexed. "That's great, I guess. But . . . it seems like an odd clue."

"Maybe." Michael stared at the handwritten note in the Bible. "But it's something. It's better than what we had before, which was nothing. To my recollection, this matches Kiki's handwriting. What do you think, Jono?"

"That's definitely her handwriting." Jono shifted, his hands going to his hips as his eyes traveled back and forth with thought. "So the killer had a helicopter . . ."

"Or he could be a helicopter pilot," I said. "We don't have enough facts to know."

He let out a little grunt and continued to stare off into the distance, as if deep in thought.

"What are you thinking?" Michael asked, seeming to notice Jono's body language.

"I'm just trying to think of who Krista might have known with a helicopter."

"Apparently, a lot of wealthy people in the area have them." I studied his face. "What about your family? Do they have one?"

I was curious as to how much Jono knew about these things. It was looking less like the helicopter was a part of a business and more like it could have been something personal. At least, that was my theory after seeing the area where Annabelle had been found.

"My dad hates helicopters," Jono said. "That's not to say that we don't have friends who own them. But the water is my dad's preferred method of transportation."

"Do you know of anybody in her circle who might have had one?" Michael closed the Bible and tucked it under his arm.

"There's only one person that I can think of who ever mentioned helicopters," Jono said. "But he didn't own one. He had his license, however."

My heart pounded in my ears, as it always did when I felt like we were getting closer to answers. "Who?"

Jono visibly cringed. "I'm not pointing any fingers. I just want to make that clear."

"We'll definitely keep that in mind," Michael said. "Who are you thinking about?"

Jono swallowed hard before saying, "James Beasley."

A FEW MINUTES of silence passed before Michael blurted, "You're telling us that James Beasley is a helicopter pilot?"

Michael looked just as surprised as I felt.

"The same James Beasley who owns the sports equipment store and who coached the opposing softball team at the game last week?" Michael continued.

Jono nodded, his gaze unwavering. "He and Krista knew each other. I think they met at a party. They didn't date or anything. Not as far as I know, at least. Like I said, after we broke up, she didn't exactly spill all the details of her life to me."

"How do you know Beasley is a pilot?" I asked, wondering what the connection was between the two of them.

"He often bragged about it. Apparently, he worked as a pilot before he decided to open his own store. He used to escort politicians around town. How do you think he had the connections to end up as the coach for the opposing softball team?"

The other team had been full of politicians. I supposed that was a good question. How *had* he ended up as their coach? Maybe Jono was right.

Michael glanced at me. "He was seen at the complex the night Velma disappeared."

"But he was supposedly picking up a date," I said. "I confirmed with the woman that it happened."

"What if, after he brought this other woman back, he and Velma crossed paths?" Michael suggested. "We don't know with 100 percent certainty that Velma disappeared around ten thirty. What if it was later on that evening?"

My chest tightened. I wanted answers. Yet, sometimes, the answers seemed so horrible. "I suppose it's a possibility worth exploring."

"We're going to need to talk to Mr. Lawson about keeping this Bible." Michael held it up. "We need to take it to the police and see if the proper authorities can make anything out of it. Either way, it could be evidence."

"You two really know what you're doing, don't you?" Jono glanced at Michael and me again, surprise laced in the depths of his gaze.

"We're trying," I said.

I just hoped we didn't let Velma down. Because I wouldn't be able to live with that fact.

CHAPTER TWENTY-EIGHT

MICHAEL DROVE when we left the Lawsons. It was just as well. Traffic was picking up, and I hated driving on the Capital Beltway at this time of day.

We dropped Jono off at his car, and he waved goodbye. He hadn't been entirely unpleasant as he'd buddied around with us. He and Michael had been cordial, so that was another blessing.

We'd already called Hunter, told him about the notation in the Bible, and he'd asked us to drop it off at the station for him.

We'd also told him about Beasley. That was when he'd started to sound excited. He said he was going to go talk to the man.

Instead of heading back to the office, Michael made a detour to Beasley's store.

When we pulled up, four police cruisers were already in the parking lot, and Hunter stood outside talking to three men in suits.

The FBI, no doubt.

As we walked up, Hunter excused himself and met us. His frown didn't indicate good news.

"Apparently, Beasley is away on a vacation," Hunter told us before we could ask any questions.

That sounded suspicious.

"Was this something last minute?" I asked.

"That's how it appears."

"Are you still on the case?" Michael asked.

"I'm helping the FBI, but they're in charge. I'm just glad I wasn't shut out completely."

That was good news because I felt certain the FBI wouldn't be inclined to share any updates with us.

"I assure you that we're going to do everything that we can to locate Beasley right now," Hunter continued. "The FBI is sending someone to his house as we speak."

"I hope you find him," I said.

Hunter glanced at my hand. "Is that the Bible?"

I handed it to him. Michael and I had put it in a paper bag, just in case there was any other evidence on it that shouldn't be disturbed.

"I've said this before, but I want to say it again." Hunter's gaze met mine then Michael's. "Good work. We appreciate all your help in this."

"I don't suppose you're any closer to finding Velma?" I asked, trying to restrain my hope.

Hunter's lips pulled into a tight line. "We're doing all that we can. I like to think we're getting closer all the time."

"I hope so," I told him.

He glanced at me again and offered a nod of reassurance. I knew Hunter. I knew he was working hard and that he wanted to find this guy more than anybody.

Michael and I waved goodbye before heading back to the office. I knew Michael needed to get home to Chloe.

And Roxy.

My throat tightened at the thought of her.

Was this the right opportunity to tell him what I'd seen?

I still wasn't sure.

Maybe I needed to do some more research on that address first.

But, if that was the right thing to do, then why did I feel so guilty?

I WAS SURPRISED when we parked behind the office and Michael just sat there lost in thought.

I paused beside my open door—I'd climbed out

because I intended on going into the office—and stared at him. "Don't you need to get home?"

"My parents picked up Chloe," he said. "I asked them to watch her for a little while. I figured I could put in a few more hours—researching Coach Beasley, to be specific. We don't have any time to waste with this case—we need to find Velma."

I couldn't argue with that.

"If you're sure." I didn't want Michael to stay just because of me. I had no obligations waiting for me at home.

Except my mom and sister.

My heart sagged. Should I be with them? I wasn't sure what good it would do. My mom worked all the time, and my sister was usually with her friends. The last time I'd gone home early to spend time with them, no one had been there.

He climbed out of the van and joined me on the other side of his van. As he did, I closed my door and leaned against the vehicle.

"I'm sure." Michael turned toward me. "I miss you, Elliot. I miss *us*."

My heart sagged at the words. The truth was I missed us too. "Me too."

He tucked a lock of hair out of my eyes and behind my ear as he studied my face. "You really are beautiful. You know that, don't you?"

I shrugged. I knew I wasn't the drop-dead gorgeous type. My figure was boyish, and I'd never win any awards for my fashion tastes.

"What makes you even more beautiful is the fact that you don't know it," Michael murmured. "And the fact that you have a heart of gold."

My heart pounded in my ears, each beat beckoning me to hold onto this thing between us forever.

More than anything I wanted to step closer. I wanted to feel Michael's arms around me. I wanted the thrill of excitement as his lips met mine.

But then I remembered Roxy.

I remembered Chloe.

I remembered the potential life-threatening brain tumor.

I couldn't pretend those things weren't happening.

I licked my lips and asked the question that had been lingering in my mind. "Michael, are you and Roxy going to try to make it work?"

A shadow crossed over his face, and he shook his head. "That's what she wants. To live the last few months of her life like a family. She wants me to forgive her."

"And what do you want?" My heart pounded harder in my ears as I waited for his answer. Forgiveness was a beautiful thing . . . but forgiveness also looked different than what we sometimes thought. Did it mean getting back together?

I wasn't sure.

"I want you," he said, his voice raspy with emotion.

I waited, sensing there was a *but* in there. As if to confirm that, Michael frowned.

"I also feel like Chloe needs to spend time with Roxy."

"That's not a terrible idea," I told him quietly.

That same grief still played out across his face. He was torn between wanting to do the right thing and trying to figure out what that right thing was. It was a hard position to be in.

Michael started to pull me closer when I stopped him. A question kept pounding me, and I knew I couldn't rest until I asked it.

"Has Roxy asked you for money?" I blurted, studying his face.

Michael twisted his head, surprise filling his gaze. "No. Why would you ask that?"

I shrugged, trying to play it off as a mindless question. "Just curious."

Based on the way Michael narrowed his eyes, he wasn't buying that explanation.

Before he could ask any more questions, his phone rang. He dropped his hand from my arm and let out a sigh.

"One minute." He pulled his phone from his pocket, glanced at the screen, and frowned. "It's Roxy."

"Go ahead and take the call."

A few minutes later, Michael finished talking to her and put his phone away. "She's not feeling well and asked if I could pick up some medicine for her at the store. She should be back at my house within the next thirty minutes."

Disappointment stretched inside me. So much for working together tonight to find out where Velma had gone.

But, instead of letting those emotions show, I nodded and stepped back. "Do what you have to do."

One day, what would happen if I didn't do the noble thing? What if I decided to start fighting for what I wanted?

That was something I was going to need to consider.

Right after we found Velma.

CHAPTER TWENTY-NINE

I WENT BACK into the office—I was the only one there
—and typed in the address of the house where I'd seen
Roxy go earlier today.

It belonged to someone named Terrence Smith.

The name didn't ring any bells with me, so I did a
quick social media search on him.

From what I could gather, the man was in his early
thirties and had spiky, dirty-blond hair and green eyes.
He worked for some type of financial institution that I'd
never heard of, liked to party, and especially liked to party
on his boat. Again, that was just based on his social media
photos.

That still didn't tell me what Roxy had been doing at
his place.

Nor did it tell me what she was doing at his place

when she was supposed to be receiving treatments for her brain tumor.

I leaned back in my desk chair as I tried to think that through.

"You look like you just lost your best friend," someone muttered.

I nearly jumped out of my seat.

I looked up and saw Oscar standing in the doorway. It was a good thing he wasn't a snake because he would have bitten me, as my mom would say.

"I didn't know you were here," I muttered, running a hand through my hair. "I didn't see your car outside when we pulled up."

"I parked across the street. Some idiot was blocking the drive when I got here. Anyway, I've been in my office. You obviously didn't realize that because you're a little bit distracted, I'd say."

I didn't bother to deny it. "I guess I am."

He crossed his thick arms and leaned against the doorway. "Thinking about Velma?"

"Yes. Velma and other stuff."

He raised an eyebrow. "Like Michael?"

My eyes widened. Did Oscar know there was something between us? I opened my mouth to speak, but then closed it again. I didn't know what to say—not if I wanted to keep my job.

"I know his ex is back," Oscar continued. "Are you worried about her too?"

I released the air from my lungs. He wasn't talking about Michael and me.

He was talking about Roxy.

Good old Roxy.

"I am concerned," I admitted.

"I am too. That's why I did a little background check on her."

I blinked in surprise—and delight. "You did? What did you discover?"

"For starters, she's never been in rehab. For the past several years, she was in Hollywood, trying to make it as an actress."

"Really?" I couldn't keep the shock from my voice.

"Really. Michael also told me about the brain tumor she supposedly has."

"You're doubtful?" I nibbled on my bottom lip as I waited for his response.

"I am."

I squirmed before divulging what I knew. "I accidentally followed her this morning."

Oscar stared at me and twisted his head. "Accidentally?"

"It's a long story. But she didn't go to treatment like she told Michael. She went to someone's house instead."

Oscar raised his eyebrows, his confusion disappearing. "You have an address?"

"I do."

"Maybe we should go check this place out."

"Together?" Certainly, I hadn't heard him correctly. Oscar and I never did anything together. We definitely didn't investigate as a team.

"Together." He nodded toward the door. "Let's go."

OSCAR DROVE. I'd never ridden with him before, and he was as terrible a driver as I'd thought he'd be. He braked too suddenly, turned too sharply, and accelerated like a jaguar darting after prey.

I hated to admit just how awkward I felt being alone with the man. Oscar had always been the man in the distance, not the man on the streets with me.

I would put that aside for the sake of Michael and Velma, though.

I'd told Oscar where we needed to go, and he'd typed the address into his GPS. As the miles rolled past, a moment of silence fell.

"Roxy is the reason Michael and I met, you know," Oscar finally said.

"Is that right?" Michael had mentioned something

about that not long ago, but he hadn't shared many details.

"He was so torn up after she left. Going from being a single guy to being a dad? It was a big change. But Michael rose to the occasion."

"And he hired you to find out if Chloe was really his, right?" That had been my understanding.

Oscar nodded. "That's right. And she is his. Michael is a different person than he used to be. Being a dad really changed him, made him grow up."

"Do you think he still loves Roxy?" The question burned my lips as the words left my mouth. Did I really want to know? Only if the answer was a resounding no.

Which meant I should have never asked.

"I can't see it." Oscar drummed his fingers on the steering wheel. "Michael is very loyal to those in his inner circle. But once you break his trust, you're out. Caput. Gone."

"But you think it's suspicious that Roxy showed up again? You must if you researched her." I really wanted to know what Oscar was thinking.

"When I first looked into Roxy, it was only a year or so after she left Michael. Back then, nothing showed up in my search. I was trying to give her the benefit of the doubt that maybe she'd gone into rehab at some point. But I didn't see any evidence of that, and I did a thorough search."

"Why would she come back? Why would she lie?"

Oscar glanced at me. "There are a lot of reasons that people lie, Elliot. I know you like to see the good in people. But not everybody does things for noble reasons."

I wasn't naïve enough to think that, even if I wanted it to be true. Life had been giving me an accelerated course in identifying people with macabre motives lately. "If you had to throw out some of those reasons, what would they be?"

"The only reason Roxy would come back was if she wanted something. She may claim that what she wants is to have a relationship with Chloe. I'm not so sure that's true, though." Oscar frowned as he stared out the front window.

"Michael said she hasn't asked for money. That's a good sign, right?"

"There are three reasons that most crimes are committed," Oscar said. "I'm sure Michael's been over them with you. The first is money. So many things boil down to people wanting wealth. The second thing is love. People do crazy things in the name of love—like, they totally lose their minds because of it. And the third reason is power. Some people just like to be in control. They feed off that feeling and need more and more of it."

"So which one of those fits Roxy?"

Oscar glanced at me. "That's what we need to figure out."

CHAPTER THIRTY

I STARED at the house I'd seen Roxy walk into earlier. It appeared that no one was home. No lights were on in the windows, and no cars sat in the driveway.

It almost looked like we'd come all the way out here for nothing.

Oscar put his car in Park and stared at the place. "What did you find out about the guy who owns this place? Terrence Whatever."

I told him what I read on the man's social media.

"And you said Roxy was supposed to go in for treatment this morning?"

"That's what she told Michael."

Oscar's eyes narrowed. "So why did she come here?"

"That's what I want to know. She apparently doesn't

know anyone else in town. That's why she's staying with Michael."

Oscar glanced at me, something changing in his gaze. "Do I detect some jealousy in your voice?"

I sucked in a quick breath. Was I that obvious?

"Jealousy?" I tried to brush him off with a laugh.

"I know you and Michael have grown close. I can see it by the way you talk to each other."

I swallowed hard, not wanting to get either Michael or myself into trouble. "Michael has become a good friend. I don't want to see anything bad happen to him."

Oscar grunted. "You know I wasn't a detective for all those years because I had no skills of observation."

"What are you saying?" I glanced at him, holding my breath as I waited for his response.

"I'm not saying anything. Just that I can tell both of you are fond of each other."

I didn't say anything for fear of saying the wrong thing and getting fired. I'd kept this job for several weeks—that was apparently a record for Oscar's new hires.

But it wasn't too late to change that.

"Where is Michael now?" Oscar asked.

I released the breath I'd been holding. He'd changed the subject—thankfully. "He was going to stay late and work, but Roxy called and said that she needed him. She wasn't feeling well from the treatments and needed him to pick up some medicine. Is there a way to find out if she really went to the hospital today?"

"There are a lot of hospitals around here, and not every treatment is done at a hospital. We *could* ask around, but it would be time-consuming, and, because of HIPAA laws, we probably wouldn't be able to find out the information we wanted."

"You're probably right. I'm going to keep trying to track down as much information as I can about her background. You said she tried to make it in Hollywood?" I repeated, still trying to think that through.

Oscar nodded. "I tracked down some sources who told me that she moved there to try to find her big break. She wasn't successful."

But something drove her back here to Storm River. Something that wasn't a life-threatening illness. I felt confident of that.

But how was I going to find out exactly what it was? And how was I going to break this news to Michael?

———

AFTER OSCAR DROPPED me back off at my car, Hunter called.

"I was hoping to catch you," he started.

I locked my doors—just to be on the safe side—and then sat there a moment. "Is everything okay?"

"I need to talk to you. Can you meet me down by the docks near The Board Room?"

My heart pounded harder. Hunter had a boat there, and we'd met at the location before. It probably wasn't a big deal . . . unless he was the Beltway Killer.

I need to use some wisdom here. Unless I want to disappear. Why do I feel so much fear? The current stakes were nothing at which to jeer.

"Sure," I finally said.

I'd stay out in public. Not go anywhere alone. Take all the precautions.

But as I started to drive that way, all kinds of suspicions rose in my mind.

I wished I could shake the theory that Hunter could possibly be a killer. But I couldn't. He did fit the description.

Except he didn't have a helicopter.

Nor did he have a helicopter license—not that I knew about, at least.

And he wasn't rich.

I shook my head. Maybe Hunter wasn't our guy after all.

I should feel relieved. But another part of me still felt suspicious. I'd probably continue to feel suspicious until we had some answers. It was the nature of this investigation, I supposed.

Besides, Beasley was our best suspect right now. As

much as I wanted to be out there tracking the man down, I knew there was very little I could do at this point. I needed to let the police do their jobs. I'd already fed them as much information as I could.

I put my car in Park, climbed out, and started across the gravel lot toward the water. As soon as I rounded the corner where The Board Room was located, I spotted Hunter standing by the dock.

He wore his usual detective attire—dark pants and a button-up shirt with cuffs rolled up to his elbows. He leaned against the railing, the dark water glimmering in front of him. He was the picture of handsome . . . and melancholy.

He glanced back when he heard my footsteps, and something that looked like an attempted smile tugged at his lips. "Thanks for coming."

I leaned on the railing beside him looking over the water. "It's no problem. I wasn't expecting to hear from you. I figured you would be out there looking for Beasley."

"He's in the wind."

"What does that mean exactly?" I honestly tried to figure it out based on context, but I had no clue.

"It means he's disappeared without a trace."

Of course. That made sense.

Or not.

"Do any of his friends know where he went?" I asked, hoping I wasn't overstepping by asking these questions.

Hunter shook his head. "No, he didn't even tell any of them that he was leaving."

"Seems like a red flag, doesn't it?"

He nodded stiffly, the lines on his face seeming to deepen. "Sure does. We were only able to find out all that information because of your hard work. Thank you. You're pretty good at this job. I still stand behind what I told you when we first met. You should look into signing up for police academy, becoming official."

"I'm pretty happy where I am right now." I knew this wasn't what he had called me over to say. But I wasn't sure where this conversation would go.

"I don't know how this case is going to turn out." Hesitation laced his voice, like he was trying to prep me or something.

"You have a lot of people on it—including the FBI," I said. "We have to keep hope alive—for Velma's sake. For Kate's sake. Dead or alive, she needs justice."

Hunter stared at me a moment. "Is there anything else you need to tell me?"

I thought about what I'd learned today. I'd told him all of it already. And something about the way he asked that question put me on edge. Did he not trust me?

"No," I finally said. "Why?"

He shrugged. "There's always been tension between

private eyes and police detectives. I just want to make sure that we're on the same team."

I wasn't sure where this was coming from, but I knew I needed to reassure him. "We both want to find Velma and stop this guy. There's no competition. Besides, I'm not getting paid by anyone to do any of this. I have no incentive to solve this before you do. I just want to know that Velma is okay."

Hunter stared at me another moment before nodding. "Okay. Thank you."

"Is that why you called me out here?"

He turned and looked out over the water. Something about his demeanor made my heart ache for him. He'd been through so much.

I placed my hand on his back. "I know this has to be incredibly difficult for you, Hunter. I'm so sorry."

He barely reacted. "I just keep thinking about what Kate went through in her final moments. I can hardly stomach it."

"We're going to get this guy. No one is going to rest until we do."

"Just one more thing to love about you." He glanced up and gave me a slight smile.

I knew I needed to be careful here. I didn't want to send the wrong signals. And again, I wasn't 100 percent sure where Michael and I stood either. Why did love have to be so complicated?

Not that I was in love.

But dating. Romance. Men.

Life would be so much simpler without any of those things present.

But I supposed it wouldn't be nearly as much fun. At least, in the end it wouldn't be.

In the end, I hoped to get the guy. The one I wanted to spend the rest of my life with. I wanted to have kids. A home. Annual family vacations. Walls of pictures full of memories.

"Remind me—did you say Krista, or Kiki as her friends called her—planned to work as a receptionist in New York?"

I started to answer but stopped myself. Because I felt fairly certain I hadn't mentioned that to Hunter at all. If that was the case, then how did he know?

I had to react carefully right now. "Yes, that's what I heard."

He nodded slowly, thoughtfully.

But a shiver went up my spine. How had he known that?

"Say, any chance you want to go for a boat ride?" Hunter stared at me, waiting for my answer.

A boat ride? I'd gone on one with him before. It had been innocent.

But now that I was considering the fact that he might

be the Beltway Killer, I knew that would be a huge mistake.

"You know what? I would, but I need to get home to my mom and sister." I took a step away. "Maybe . . . another time."

He reached for me, but I stepped out of his grip. Terror rushed through me.

Could Hunter have been the guy who'd picked up Annabelle? Had Kate died because she'd discovered Hunter's secret identity?

I didn't know. But I couldn't chance it.

"I'm sorry," I stuttered. "I've got to go, though."

Before he could touch me again, I fled to my car.

What if I'd just been face-to-face with a serial killer?

CHAPTER THIRTY-ONE

NOT GETTING any sleep the night before had left me more exhausted than I thought. Suddenly, now that darkness had fallen, all I wanted was to get home and rest.

And forget about Hunter.

Had I overreacted? I wasn't sure.

Another part of me felt guilty because life felt painfully normal.

If Velma couldn't be safe and comfortable, then why should I? Yet I knew I'd be no good to this investigation if I didn't get some slumber. I would think more clearly if I was able to rest, even if for just a bit.

But when I walked into my house, I sensed something was wrong.

It started when I heard my sister coughing.

And coughing.

And coughing some more.

She wasn't doing okay.

As they came into view, I saw my mom standing beside Ruth at the kitchen table. She rubbed my sister's back as Ruth wore a special vest that helped loosen the mucus in her chest.

Concern rose inside me.

How much longer could Ruth go on like this? How much longer until she got that lung transplant she needed?

"I tried to call you." Disappointment lined my mom's voice as she stared at me, heat in her eyes.

I glanced at my phone and saw that I *had* missed several calls from her. "When I slid my phone into my pocket, it must have rubbed against my jeans and flipped the button into silent mode. That happened the other day too. I'm sorry."

My mom didn't seem to hear me—or maybe she just didn't care. "Your sister isn't doing well."

The agitation in her voice made me flinch. I wasn't used to things being this rocky between us, and I hated the feeling.

I sat down beside my sister and squeezed her hand.

She pulled away.

Rejection.

Ruth wanted me to know loud and clear how she felt about what I was doing.

I wasn't going to win here, was I?

"I thought we were always there for each other," my sister said, coughing again.

"I am always here for you. I'm sorry, but my phone was on silent. You know that's not a normal thing for me."

"You're still trying to find that serial killer, aren't you?" She stared at me—or was it more of a glare?

"I'm still trying to find my friend. But I'm working with the police and not doing anything foolish. I promise."

"Did you drive home by yourself?" My mom stared at me, waiting for my answer.

I resisted a sigh, knowing I'd been caught. "I did, but—"

"Then you are doing foolish things," my mom finished. "You shouldn't go anywhere by yourself. Not with a serial killer out there."

"Mom—" I stopped myself.

There was nothing I could say to her. Nothing that would convince her that I was being smart.

Tensions were too high right now, as were emotions. Besides, what was it my dad always said? You could win an argument but lose the war. That's what this felt like. There were deeper issues at stake, deeper than me trying to find this killer.

But none of us wanted to talk about our grief after Dad's death. At least, that's how it seemed to me.

"Do you need to go to the doctor?" I turned my attention back to Ruth.

She shook her head, but her features looked haggard. "I'm fine. I just need to let the vest do its job. I can always count on it to help me when I need it."

That had been meant to jab at me. I had no doubt about that.

After a moment of studying her, I finally nodded. How many more times could I apologize? It wasn't going to make a difference.

Everything is falling apart. I thought moving here would be a new start. Instead, everything is battering my heart.

"Okay, then." I stood. "Well, if there's nothing else for me to do here, I'm going to turn in for the night. I'm exhausted."

No one said anything.

But I could feel their eyes on me as I walked away.

And I hated the tension between us more than I hated losing acres of rainforest to a fire.

And I really hated that.

AS SOON AS I got into my room and slipped into bed, all my exhaustion disappeared and I felt wide awake.

Of course.

Maybe I just needed to jot a few things down so my mind could rest. That usually did the trick.

I pulled out my notebook and studied everything I knew about the killer, careful to add my new notes about Krista.

The woman had left with all her things. Her car was gone. But no one had heard from her, and she'd left that weird notation in the Bible by her bed.

If Hunter or Beasley weren't the killer—and there was a chance they weren't—then who else could be? Were there any more suspects worth considering?

I remembered that table of pictures I'd passed at Lawson's house. There had been a man in one of the photos. He'd had dark hair and a bright smile.

I was pretty sure he'd been wearing a military uniform.

I nibbled on the side of my lip. On impulse, I did some quick research on the family. A few clicks later, I discovered that Lawson had a nephew named Nolan Reid. From what I could tell, the man was in the Navy.

Which meant he'd know how to tie a nautical knot like the one that had been tied around the rose—the Beltway Killer's calling card.

But that wasn't enough to make him a suspect.

Had Nolan and Krista ever met?

I typed in a few more things and discovered that Mr.

Lawson had posted lots of pictures of his and his wife's travels. I compared the dates on some of the photos.

Many of the times they were out of town were when the victims had disappeared.

But they were in town now. And Velma was missing. So that theory didn't make much sense.

I shook my head. Maybe this was too much of a reach.

I needed to sleep on it, I supposed.

Meanwhile, I still wondered if the Beltway Killer had some affiliation with the houses in the area where Michael and I had been today.

If Annabelle truly had heard a helicopter, then the location should have a helipad, right? I didn't know much about these things, but it made sense.

Excitement pulsed through me.

Maybe I was onto something.

I found some satellite images online and began to look at the aerial views of the area.

But thirty minutes later, I had nothing.

Trees obscured some of the landscape. Though a helipad shouldn't be beneath a tree, I still didn't see anything that indicated one was hiding just out of sight.

I was back to square one, it appeared.

I frowned.

That wasn't where I wanted to be.

I wanted Velma to be found. The Beltway Killer to be

THE SKILL OF SNOOPING   255

caught. Michael and I to figure out our future. Roxy to be exposed. My sister to have that lung transplant.

And my father's potential killer to be brought to justice.

Why did it feel like everything was starting to fall apart and that answers were remaining just out of reach?

CHAPTER THIRTY-TWO

TODAY WAS the day I had to tell Michael the truth about Roxy. I just had to find the right time to do so. That was my goal when I woke up that morning.

I should have told Michael yesterday. I shouldn't have been so wishy-washy.

Today, I wouldn't talk myself out of it. No matter what.

I walked into the office and immediately spotted Michael. He sat at his desk, staring at his computer.

As he looked at me, his gaze brightened for a moment. "How's it going, Elliot?"

"It's going." I didn't know what else to say without pouring out all my problems—which wasn't what I wanted to do. I paused near my desk and looked at him. "Any progress with the case?"

He shook his head and leaned back in his chair. "Not yet. You?"

"I spent last night looking at aerial photographs of the area where Annabelle was found. Specifically, I was looking for a helipad. I couldn't tell anything from the photos, unfortunately."

Michael sat up slightly. "You know, I think you could be onto something."

"I was hoping that was the case. We can't exactly search house to house to see who has a helipad. Besides, you probably don't even have to have a permit to build one so it's not like we could go to the city records either."

Michael rubbed his jaw, his eyes drifting in thought. "But I think there could be another way."

Now he had my attention. "What are you thinking?"

"I'm thinking we use a drone."

Well, that was certainly an interesting idea. "Can you fly one?"

"As a matter of fact, Oscar sent me to a course last year so I could learn how to do just that. I haven't had very many opportunities to put my new skills into action. But I think that this just might be our ideal time."

My heart lifted with anticipation. "Then what are we waiting for?"

"I like how you think. Let me grab the drone, and we can go."

FLUTTERS TICKLED my stomach as Michael and I headed down the road.

Just tell him, an internal voice said.

Yet, I was having trouble doing so. If only I had some concrete evidence to prove Roxy was up to something. But I didn't.

I just needed to approach this very carefully.

"What's Roxy doing today?" I finally started.

"She's resting at my place."

The flutters in my stomach turned to a growl of nausea. "Is she?"

"Unfortunately, yes. I guess this radiation makes her tired. She's trying to be strong, but ..."

If this case wasn't so pressing, I might have tried to follow Roxy again this morning. But I'd nearly slept through my alarm, which totally wasn't like me. I'd just barely gotten here in time.

"How did things go last night?" I almost didn't want to ask the question, yet I couldn't stop myself either.

"Chloe loves having Roxy there, and Roxy seems to really love Chloe. It's weird to see how quickly they bonded. But I guess that's what happens with blood relatives sometimes."

"And you?"

He nodded slowly, thoughtfully. "I was there with them. Watching. Trying to figure things out."

"And were you successful?"

His lips pulled into a taut line. "I wish the answer was yes. But I wasn't."

I leaned back, possibly delaying the inevitable, possibly collecting more information. "How did the two of you even meet?"

"At a club. I'm not proud of it. But I'm not the person that I used to be either."

Michael had always been very open about the mistakes he'd made in his past. A person's history didn't bother me nearly as much as a person's current actions did. We all needed grace in our lives and had made mistakes in our pasts. Me included.

Sometimes, I was at the top of that list.

I cleared my throat. "Does Roxy seem . . . the same?"

Michael shrugged. "Not really. I think she's grown up some, and she really wants to be a part of Chloe's life. Facing a life-threatening illness can do that, I suppose."

"How are you feeling about Chloe and Roxy bonding?" I was pretty good at dancing around the fire like I didn't have a guinea pig to roast. Yes, I loved that expression.

He rubbed his jaw. "Not great. I'm trying to work through it. It's hard to say no to a dying woman."

And that was probably exactly what Roxy was banking on.

I opened my mouth to tell him what I knew, but, before the words came out, Michael's phone rang. It was Oscar, calling to check in for the day.

Just as the call ended, we pulled into a community park.

We left Michael's minivan in a lot there and trotted toward the woods in the distance, away from anyone on the playground who might see us.

A few minutes later, Michael successfully launched the drone into the air. A screen stretched in the middle of the controller, showing us everything from the camera on the bottom of the device.

Now I could only pray that we would actually find something.

CHAPTER THIRTY-THREE

I STOOD CLOSE TO MICHAEL, enjoying the feeling of his body heat a little too much. But I had a good reason to brush arms with him.

I needed to watch the screen also. Two sets of eyes were better than one.

I'd printed off a map of the area so I could cross off each property as we surveilled it. It seemed like the best way to get this done and to track what we were doing.

"How long can we keep this drone in the air?" I asked, never having used one of these things before.

"We should have about thirty minutes, at least. After that, I'll have to bring her back and change the batteries."

With an expertise that surprised me, Michael flew the device over the properties. We were able to mark off four locations right away. With those, the lots were large, but there was clearly nowhere to land a helicopter. They'd been too wooded, too crowded.

"Is this legal?" I asked.

"It's complicated. You can't legally use them to spy on private property. Some cities in the area, like Arlington, have also banned them."

"So we could get in trouble?"

"Let's hope not. Sometimes it's better to ask forgiveness than permission."

That wasn't comforting.

"These are some nice houses," I muttered, looking at the stately structures and trying to put my mind at ease.

"Tell me about it. Who really needs a house that big?"

"Somebody who wants people to know that they're important?"

Michael let out a little chuckle. "You could be right. I like the way you think."

"I really hope we find something."

"Me too." A new somberness entered his tone.

It had been too long since Velma disappeared. Even though we'd found some clues and were getting closer to answers, I had to wonder if we were moving fast enough to save our friend.

I didn't know the answer to that question.

And I wasn't okay with that.

An hour later, the drone was still flying, and Michael and I had marked off a majority of the properties. But the task was beginning to feel never-ending. The area was larger than I'd envisioned.

If Annabelle had escaped from one of these houses, she was unsure how far she'd run. Would it have been for hours? Doubtful.

To her recollection, her escape had been through the woods. But she'd also been drugged, so her memories were foggy.

What if we were wasting time and looking in the wrong direction? I didn't want to think like that. I needed to stay positive.

"Maybe we should consider the possibility that there isn't a helipad," I muttered. "Maybe all you really need is a decent sized patch of grass or even a tennis court or a large driveway."

Michael shrugged. "I suppose we could expand our search to that."

Just then, his phone rang.

"Can you pull it from my pocket?" Michael said, glancing over his shoulder.

I stared at his back pocket. "Isn't that weird?"

"I trust that you're not going to take advantage of me." He shot me a look.

I let out a quick, nervous chuckle and carefully took it out of his back pocket. Then I showed him the screen.

He frowned.

It was Roxy calling.

"Would you mind answering and putting it on speaker?" Michael asked. "I just need to know that there's not an emergency."

"Sure thing." I hit the button but dreaded listening to the conversation.

A moment later, Roxy's voice came on the line. "Hey, Mikey."

Mikey?

I resisted the urge to gag.

"How are you doing, Roxy?" Michael asked. "Feeling okay?"

"Not great. I'm feeling a little nauseous, unfortunately."

"I am sorry to hear that."

"Me too. Listen, I know your parents are picking up Chloe from school. But I wondered if, once she got to their house, if I might take her for ice cream? I'd like to spend some more time with her."

Alarm raced through me when I heard her words.

"Just you and her?" Michael asked as if he was considering it.

"I thought it could be some fun bonding. Plus, it would give me something to look forward to. I could use that right about now."

Michael opened his mouth, and, in my gut, I knew he was going to say yes.

All my doubts about Roxy surged to the surface.

What if she didn't just want to take Chloe to get ice cream? What if she wanted to run away with Chloe? What if that was Roxy's plan this whole time?

"I don't see any problem with that—" Michael started.

"No!" I said. "You can't do that."

Michael turned his head toward me, confusion written in the wrinkles on his forehead. He whispered, "What are you talking about?"

"She's lying to you," I mouthed.

"What?" Michael said.

"Michael?" Roxy said. "Who's that with you?"

Michael continued to stare at me in shock. "I'm going to have to call you back, Roxy."

"Okay. I just want to let you know that this would mean a lot to me, though."

As Roxy ended the call, I pulled the phone back toward me and waited for Michael's questions. I knew he was going to have them and braced myself for how unpleasant things might turn.

"What's going on?" Michael asked. "What are you talking about?"

This was the time. I couldn't go back.

I had to tell Michael the truth.

Even if I felt sick to my stomach at the thought of it.

I SUCKED IN A DEEP BREATH, trying to give myself a mental pep talk before starting.

I had to put my own desires and emotions aside and do what was best for Michael and Chloe. That's what all of this boiled down to.

"I went past your house the other day because I wanted to tell you something," I started. "Except, when I got there, I saw Roxy leaving. Then it felt awkward. So I headed to work, which happened to be in the same direction that Roxy was driving."

"Okay . . ."

"Long story short, she didn't go to a hospital or medical facility. She went to somebody's house."

He squinted and glanced back at the remote then at me again. "You followed her?"

"Not on purpose. Not at first at least. I guess I just got curious."

His gaze darkened. "Whose house exactly did she go to?"

"I have no idea. Someone named Terrence Smith. I did some research on him and found out he's a finance guy. That was all I could find out about him online."

"You researched him?" he echoed.

I nodded, knowing there was no need to hold anything back now. I had already jumped off the deep end. "Oscar and I both did."

"What?" Michael's voice rose with surprise.

"We're both worried about you. We think it's suspicious that Roxy is back in your life right now. Besides that, Oscar discovered that she never checked herself into any type of drug rehab."

"You guys have researched that also?" Michael stared at me, but I couldn't read his expression.

I couldn't tell if he was angry or relieved or curious or … what.

"I didn't. Oscar researched that."

Michael let out a sigh and glanced back at the drone screen again. "If you were so worried, why didn't you let me know earlier?"

This was where it got even more uncomfortable. "Because I knew how it would sound. Like I was jealous or something. I wanted you to be able to make your own choices. I didn't want to be one of those girls who sounded like a backstabber."

"But Chloe is involved here." His voice made it clear he was not happy.

I couldn't blame him, not when he reminded me of that fact.

I lowered my tone to just above a whisper. "I know she is, and you've got to know how much I care about Chloe. I didn't know what to do. I've been sick to my stomach as I've tried to figure out if I needed to tell you or not. I wasn't sure how well you would take to me getting into your business."

His gaze remained narrow, and he stiffly shook his head. "You should have told me."

"Michael, I don't know what Roxy is up to, but it's not good. Please don't let Chloe go anywhere alone with her. If you do, I fear what might happen to her."

Just as I said the words, his hand slipped from the controller.

The next thing we knew, the remote showed the drone crashing into the woods.

CHAPTER THIRTY-FOUR

MICHAEL MUTTERED something under his breath. "There went a ten thousand-dollar piece of equipment."

My eyebrows shot up. "That thing cost that much?"

Michael nodded, though the motion looked heavy. "Yep. Oscar isn't going to be happy. I'm going to have to go get it."

"Really?" I knew it made sense, but that was entirely more complicated than flying it overhead. I glanced at the map in my hands.

"Have any idea where it just went down?"

Using my finger, I followed the path the device had taken. I stopped on one of the lots. "It should be in here somewhere."

"Let's see if we can drive any closer. Then we're going to have to take a hike. Hope you're ready for it."

I was ready for anything—except for Michael to cut me out of his life.

As we trudged past the playground back to his minivan, I turned to him. "I'm sorry, Michael."

This was all my fault. I'd distracted him from his job by telling him about Roxy.

I felt like I couldn't do anything right lately. Shouldn't I be past this point in my life? Or did everyone have moments like this, when everything that was important felt like it had been turned upside down?

"You don't have to be sorry." Michael's words contradicted his tone, which sounded distant. "I just wish you had told me sooner."

"Even though it makes me seem nosy and pushy?"

"Yeah, even though." We climbed into his minivan. "I felt like something was up with Roxy. I looked into her background last night too, and I knew that she hadn't been in rehab. What I can't figure out is why she came back. I've never heard that name Terrence Smith before. I have no idea who he is."

"So you've been suspicious also?" Relief washed through me.

"I was trying to give her the benefit of the doubt, but I can see now that was a mistake."

"There's no way that she can pick up Chloe from school or anything, is there?"

He shook his head as we started down the road, trying to find a spot closer to the drone. "No, they have a very strict policy at the elementary school campus. But this does make me nervous. In fact, I'm going to call my parents and the school just to make sure that nobody else picks up Chloe except my parents. I don't want there to be any confusion."

"Sounds like a good idea." A flutter of nerves went through me.

I didn't want to see Michael get hurt. But I *really* didn't want to see Chloe get hurt either. Especially not through the scenarios that played out in my mind.

Michael put his phone on Bluetooth as he made the calls.

When he finished, he looked a little more at ease. But I knew that more than anything he probably wanted Chloe to stay at his side and remain there until he knew she was safe. That's how I would feel if I had a daughter.

"I wonder if Roxy really is sick or not." Michael shook his head, his gaze looking far off. "She's a good actress."

"Well, she did go to Hollywood for a while and try to make it big."

He jerked his gaze toward me. "She did?"

"That's what Oscar said."

Michael shook his head and let out a bitter chuckle. "Just what is she up to?"

"As soon as we find this drone, maybe we can figure that out."

He pulled off on the side of the road and put his van into Park. "Yes, we'll have to do that. For now, let's go find the drone."

I TRIED to keep track of the path Michael and I were taking through the woods. Hopefully, we weren't caught trespassing because a trip to jail wouldn't exactly expedite the process of getting to Chloe any sooner, finding out any more answers about Roxy, or locating Velma.

While we were walking, my phone rang. When I saw my mom's name on the screen, I knew I had to answer—especially after the issues we'd had yesterday.

"Elliot, guess what?" My mom's voice sounded excited as it stretched over the line.

"What's going on?"

"Your sister is number two on the transplant list!"

Hope surged in me. "That's great news."

"I know, isn't it? I need to go to the hospital and meet with the team there. But they're going to want to verify that we have the funds for this."

The hope that I felt began to sink. I knew we didn't have the cash on hand that we needed in order to make this happen. I had no way of making it magically appear either.

Unless I found the Beltway Killer.

A reward had been promised to the person who offered the tip leading to his capture.

But could I do that before tomorrow? It didn't seem likely. Besides, even if this worked out, it wouldn't be just me finding him. A whole team had been working on finding him.

"We're going to figure this out," I insisted to my mom.

"We need a miracle."

"I know. But we can't give up hope yet. We're going to figure out a way to have that money and pay for her surgery."

"I hope so, Elliot. Because your sister's life depends on it."

Those final words drove home just how serious this whole situation was.

More than one person's life was on the line right now.

For that matter, it seemed like too many people's lives were on the line.

Velma.

Chloe.

Even mine.

I hated feeling helpless to do anything about it.

"Is everything okay?" Michael glanced at me.

I told him what my mom had said.

"That's great news." He continued tromping through the woods.

"It is. However, we're supposed to have our finances lined up. I'm afraid we've fallen short. If money prevents my sister from having the surgery, I don't know what we'll do."

"I'm sorry, Elliot. I have some money in my savings—"

"I couldn't ask you to give that up for us."

"You didn't ask. I offered."

I glanced at him. "But you and Chloe might need that one day."

"And if we do, God will provide. Just how short are you?"

"Thirty thousand dollars."

"With my added twenty thousand, then you would only need ten thousand more."

I still didn't feel right taking money from Michael. But if it meant my sister could have surgery, then I didn't know how I could refuse. Either way, we still wouldn't have enough.

The dilemma caused my muscles to pull taut inside me.

"You're going to have the money in time," Michael said. "I just know it."

I hoped he was right.

And I hoped we could find this drone. I didn't have the money to pay Oscar back for it.

And now we didn't have a device to help us search the area in hopes of finding Velma.

More pressure pushed on me at the thought.

How were we going to locate her now?

CHAPTER THIRTY-FIVE

"HERE'S THE DRONE." Michael lifted it from a tangle of branches and vines.

One of the arms was bent and a propeller dangled by a wire.

I frowned. "You think it's fixable?"

As soon as I said the word, the propeller dropped to the ground. I scooped it up and pushed it into my pocket.

Michael shrugged. "Everything is fixable. The question is how much it will cost."

I frowned. "What now?"

"Now we head back and figure out our next step."

I looked in the distance and saw some property. "While we're here, we might as well peek at this house. At least I can cross it off my list."

Michael shrugged, and we walked over to the edge of the woods.

Just like the other homes in the area, this one was huge. It had towers and turrets and big porches. The stone exterior made it look a bit like a fairy tale castle.

I grabbed Michael's arm. "Do you see that?"

"See what?"

"The top of that garage. It's flat."

"You mean like a landing pad?" Michael asked.

"Exactly. It would be hard to tell the dimensions of that looking at the aerial photographs. But here looking at it face on, it's clear."

"You might be onto something." Michael glanced around again. "Woods surround this property. If Annabelle was here, I could see where it would feel like she ran through the forest for a long time before she finally hit the road."

"Any idea who lives here?"

"No idea."

I turned toward him, my heart pounding in my chest. "Do you think this could be it? Do you think Velma could be here?"

"All we're going off of is the location where Annabelle was found, as well as having a space that's big enough for a helicopter." Michael stared at the property in the distance. "It doesn't seem like quite enough evidence, does it?"

I grabbed Michael's arm. "Do you see that?"

"What am I looking at?"

"That truck. You can barely see it on the other side of the property. But it's an old Ford. Just like the one—"

"That Mr. Lawson owns," Michael finished. His jaw tightened as he stared at it. "I don't like where this is going."

"Me neither." I grabbed my phone. "I have a few more questions for Jono, however."

Before Michael could stop me, I dialed his number. He answered on the first ring. "Elliot. What's going on?"

"I have a few more questions about Krista." I got right to the point. "Do you know anything about one of Mr. Lawson's nephews? A man named Nolan?"

"Yeah, as a matter of fact, I did hear his name. Just last night, for that matter."

My pulse spiked. "Really?"

"After we talked, I decided to give a few of our old friends a call. I wanted to know if they had heard from Krista. One of them told me she'd gone on a few dates with one of Mr. Lawson's nephews. A man named Nolan Reid."

I gripped the phone tighter. "What else do you know about him?"

"I heard that on every date he gave her a single red rose."

A single red rose? That information was supposed to

be classified. Only a few people knew about the flowers that had been left with the Beltway Killer's victims.

I swallowed hard, my throat suddenly feeling tight. "Anything else?"

"Get this," Jono said. "This guy was a helicopter pilot in the military."

My heart beat harder.

"Do me a favor. I don't have great service out here. Could you double-check and see what his address is?"

"Sure."

I waited for a few minutes in silence as he did that. A moment later, he came back on the line. "Two Eighty-Three Waterford Lane."

I glanced at the house in front of me.

The numbers 283 were on the side of it.

This was Nolan Reid's house.

And there was a good chance that Velma was inside.

"Jono, you need to call the FBI. Tell him everything we just talked about. They need to get their people to that address. Now."

"You really think he's our guy?"

I stared at the house. "I do."

─────────

"FOLLOW MY LEAD," Michael said as we walked toward the front door. "We don't know what kind of situation we're walking into right now or if this guy even knows who we are."

"Got it," I said.

A surge of anxiety mixed with excitement in me. I had no idea how this would play out. But my gut told me we were getting closer to finding Velma.

Michael rang the bell beside the massive double doors at the front of the house. They were painted a glossy black, and no expense had been spared.

I held my breath as I waited, anxious as to whether or not somebody would answer.

A moment later, an older gentleman, probably in his seventies, answered.

My first thought was, *The butler did it.*

Not because I thought this man actually did anything. But I didn't realize that people actually had butlers, and that's exactly who this man seemed to be.

"We're sorry to interrupt you," Michael said. "But our dog pulled away from us as we were walking him, and I think he's wandering in the woods behind your house. I was wondering if we could have your permission to look for him?"

The man observed us for a moment before nodding. "I suppose. Just make it quick."

As they talked, I glanced behind the man. The inside of the house looked stately, and I didn't see anybody else here. I certainly didn't see Mr. Lawson.

Where was he? Had he been lying to us the whole time yesterday? Did he know what his nephew was up to?

"Thank you so much, sir," Michael said. "We will stay out of your hair."

With a final nod, we started toward the backyard of the massive estate.

"Missing dog, huh?" I said, trying to keep in step with Michael.

"Works like a charm every time."

"Are we really going to search the woods?"

"Maybe a little. But this will give us a chance to get closer to the home. Looking at it, it definitely has a basement. And you're right. That area on top of the garage could very easily be a helipad. This could be our place. Velma could be here."

"I just hope the FBI gets here in time."

"Me too. We don't have any time to waste."

Michael took my hand and pulled me along the side of the house. I kept my eyes wide open, looking for any sign that Velma had been here. But the grounds were immaculate, and the whole property was quiet.

I wanted to yell for Velma. See if she could hear me. To offer her some hope and let her know that help was here.

But I couldn't do that.

As we crossed toward the other side of the property, I clearly saw Mr. Lawson's truck.

He wasn't inside.

There was one more car here, and I had to assume that that belonged to the man who had answered the door.

"Come on." Michael tugged me into the open garage.

"We're going inside?"

"It's the only way we're going to find out if Velma is here. We just need to stay quiet."

I nodded, although a little too quickly and adamantly. "I can do that."

Michael grabbed the back doorknob and slowly twisted it.

It was unlocked.

With one last glance around, we slipped into the house.

CHAPTER THIRTY-SIX

I COULD HARDLY BREATHE as Michael and I crept into the house. A sprawling kitchen greeted us, complete with streamlined appliances, marble countertops, and a shiny wood floor.

The inside was just as quiet as the outside, I noted.

Where had the butler gone? And where had this Nolan guy gotten all this wealth? Mr. Lawson's house had been nothing like this, so it obviously wasn't family money. Could Nolan really make this kind of a salary as a helicopter pilot in the Navy?

So many questions collided inside my head, and it would take me awhile to sort through them.

I gripped Michael's hand as he led me through the kitchen toward a hallway on the other side.

I knew what he was looking for.

A door leading to the basement.

But, if I had to guess, this place was probably ten thousand square feet. Maybe more. It seemed massive.

I paused as a step sounded in the distance. Michael quickly opened a nearby door and pulled me through it. Based on the darkness, the clothes clinging to my shoulders, and the smell of moth balls, we were in a closet.

Through the crack, I saw the butler walk past with a pile of something in his hands. Dishtowels. He deposited them in the kitchen before walking back in the opposite direction.

I released the breath I held, not even realizing I'd been holding it.

That was close.

The good news was that he appeared to be walking toward the other side of the house now. That would give Michael and me the opportunity to search this side.

I only prayed that the door to the basement was closer to us than it was to the butler.

We started to step out of the closet when I heard something else.

A buzzing.

The sound came from my pocket.

My phone!

What had I been thinking? I should have put it on Silent.

I jerked it from my pocket and glanced at the screen. Jono.

"Answer it," Michael whispered.

Trying not to fumble too much, I hit Answer and put the device to my ear.

"I did a little more research," Jono said. "Get this— Nolan Reid is a decorated war hero. Though he'd often go on deployment, it looks like he was in the country every single time a new woman disappeared. I had to pull a few strings to get that information, but it was worth it."

My pulse continued to pound as I let his words wash over me.

"Thanks for letting us know, Jono," I whispered. "You've been a real lifesaver."

"I called the FBI and Hunter. They're on their way."

"Perfect."

He paused. "Why are you whispering? You didn't go try to find Velma yourself, did you?"

I swallowed hard. "I've got to go."

Before he could ask any more questions, I put my phone away.

We didn't have much time.

We needed to find Velma and get out of here.

WHEN MICHAEL and I were sure that the butler was out of sight, we crept out from the closet. I was certain to put my phone on Silent this time so we didn't have any more surprises.

Since we'd only seen two cars, did that mean that Nolan wasn't here? Was Lawson working with him, acting as his right-hand man?

These were all things I needed to be aware of.

Still, something in the back of my mind wasn't making sense. I tried to pull that realization forward, but it didn't work. My senses were too heightened now. My adrenaline pumped too hard for logic to take over.

I hoped that nagging thought would come to me soon.

"This way," Michael whispered, pointing to a hallway on our left.

We quietly crept down the corridor. As we reached a door beneath the stairway, Michael pulled on the handle.

It opened, and steps stretched downward before us.

Michael and I glanced at each other.

This was it.

The basement.

And the moment when we would find out if we were on the right track or not.

Sucking in a shaky breath, I took my first step, following behind Michael as we descended into the abyss —that's how it felt, at least.

Then I took another step.

And another.

And another.

And another.

The space around me was obviously well insulated. I could tell simply by the acoustics as I walked down. Back in Yerba, my best friend's father had been a musician and had a studio in his home. The sound in here reminded me of that.

It would be perfect for obscuring the screams of any potential victims of the Beltway Killer.

A chill washed through me at that thought.

As Michael and I reached the bottom, another hallway waited for us. Behind any one of the doors ahead we might find Velma.

I prayed that would be the case.

And, even more than that, I prayed she would be okay.

CHAPTER THIRTY-SEVEN

I COULD HARDLY BREATHE as I paused by the first door.

I twisted the handle.

It was locked.

On the other side of me, Michael did the same.

That door was also locked.

We weren't going to have much luck if it continued this way.

We tried four other doors, and they were all the same. Every single one of them was unbreachable.

Not only that, but it was strangely quiet down here. The only thing I could hear was the hum of the AC as it blew through the vents. There were no signs of life otherwise.

I turned toward Michael as we reached the end of the hallway. "What now?"

His jaw twitched, and I could tell he didn't like this new development. But if Velma was behind one of these doors, then of course it was locked. The problem was, we didn't have a key.

Michael shook his head and stepped closer to one of the doors. He leaned toward it and called, "Velma? Are you in there?"

Nothing.

He moved to the second door and did the same. Nothing again.

When he reached the sixth door, we heard a voice call back.

"Michael?"

My breath caught. Had I been hearing things or was that... Velma?

Michael leaned closer, something seeming to light inside him. "Velma? It's me. Michael."

Even with the thick door between us, I heard her crying. "You found me. I didn't think anyone would find me."

"We're going to try to get you out of here," Michael told her. "But we don't have a key, so we're going to have to get creative."

"Michael, you have to be careful. If he finds you—"

"I know," Michael said into the door. "The FBI is on

the way. Just hold tight for another minute while we figure this out."

What were we going to do?

I reached into my pocket. I had put the propeller from the drone in there. The tiny, thin pieces might fit into the lock. It seemed like it was worth a try.

Wasting no time, I stepped forward. I inserted one of the blades into the lock and began to jiggle it.

Nothing happened.

"Let me have a turn," Michael said.

I let him take over. It was just as well. My hands were too jittery right now. Besides, Michael had more experience with this kind of thing.

But I held my breath as I waited. In between doing that, I glanced down the hallway, halfway expecting to see the Beltway Killer appear.

But I saw no one. Not yet, at least.

I prayed that it remained that way.

Finally, Michael released a breath. As he stepped back, I saw the latch release.

He'd done it. He'd picked the lock.

The door opened, and Velma flew out. She collapsed into Michael's arms, and he held her up as sobs wracked her body.

I stepped closer and put my hand on her back.

I'd never been so glad to see someone.

But I knew our troubles were far from over.

We had to somehow get her out of here.

Our lives depended on it.

"ARE YOU OKAY TO WALK?" Michael studied Velma's wet, tear-laden face as he asked the question.

She quickly nodded, still clinging to him as if she couldn't stand on her own. "If it means getting out of here then yes."

Michael kept an arm around her as we started toward that stairway. So far, everything had gone smoothly. I prayed it remained that way.

But anxiety tried to grip my muscles, my thoughts, my very breath.

Could it really be this easy?

"I'm so glad you're okay," Michael muttered to Velma. "You had us all worried. Even Oscar."

A whimper escaped from her, and she flung a hand over her mouth. "I thought I was going to die."

"We weren't going to stop until we found you," Michael said.

"I knew you guys were looking." Velma glanced back at me, her face scrunched with emotion. "I knew it."

"We weren't going to give up on you," I told her. "No chance."

I quickly observed her as we continued down the

hallway. She didn't look like she'd been injured. At least on the outside. There were no bruises on her face or arms. No busted lips or cuts. She only limped slightly.

We reached the stairway, and I started up the first step. I'd check at the top to make sure that the coast was clear before Michael and Velma emerged.

After we made our way up the steps, I paused at the door and braced myself for whatever I might see on the other side.

But as I twisted the handle, it didn't move.

It was almost like the door had been . . . locked.

How was that possible?

I knew the answer, I just didn't want to face it.

"What's wrong?" Michael rushed, leaning toward me while still holding onto Velma.

"It's locked."

"What?" He reached by me to twist the handle himself.

It didn't budge for him either.

When I glanced at his face, I saw the alarm written into the tight lines there.

We both knew the truth.

Something was wrong.

I only hoped that the authorities got here before we all died.

But before I could even complete that thought, I sensed someone behind us.

I glanced down at the base of the stairs, and I saw a figure standing there.

That's when I knew that none of us would be getting out of here anytime soon.

Indeed, all of this *had* been too easy.

CHAPTER THIRTY-EIGHT

"I APPRECIATE you guys letting me know you were coming."

My eyes widened as I heard the arrogance of the words as they filled the room.

Jono Harris stood at the base of the stairs, a gun in his hands, and a dull expression in his eyes.

"Jono?" Michael's voice held just as much disbelief as I felt. "What are you doing?"

He stepped closer. "You weren't supposed to find me."

"You're the Beltway Killer?" I couldn't believe it. Yet I could.

I should have put this all together sooner. Jono had all the qualities I'd put together in my profile. I'd just assumed someone who had everything—someone like Jono—wouldn't have a reason to do something like this.

He could have and do anything he wanted.

So why resort to murder?

Velma let out another whimper beside me.

"It's not what you think." Jono's voice sounded cold, almost like he had no emotion left in him. Or no heart. Neither was comforting.

"What is it like then?" Michael asked.

"You wouldn't understand." Jono sneered at us. "Now I'm going to have to deal with you."

"What about all that information you gave us earlier?" I stepped closer, wanting to look this man in the eyes. "You were making all that information up. You wanted to make Nolan look guilty, but you knew none of it was true. You wanted to lure us here, just for this moment."

Jono's expression remained placid as he pointed his gun at me. "I knew you were getting too close to the truth. I couldn't let you go to the police with that information."

"How is keeping us here going to make anything better?" Michael asked. "People are still going to come looking for us."

"Easy. I'll make it look like a home invasion. I was simply defending myself and didn't realize that two nosy PIs were snooping at my place." He said the words as easily as he might if he were talking about taking the trash out.

"But, if you shoot us, you'll have police swarming all

THE SKILL OF SNOOPING   301

over this house," I reminded him. "They'll find evidence of what you've done here."

"Don't worry. I have a plan. I always have a plan."

Michael moved toward him, ignoring the gun in Jono's hands. "We were friends. How could you do this? How could you kill Kiki?"

A bloom of red appeared on Jono's cheeks. "I didn't want to. She just reminded me so much of my mother. She needed to be taught a lesson."

I almost wanted to roll my eyes. Not mother issues. Why did it seem like every criminal used that as their defense?

Behind me, Velma nearly collapsed on the steps. I left her there, figuring she was safer behind Michael and me than she was beside us. She was in no state to try to defend herself.

"Is Mr. Lawson here?" I asked. "We saw his truck outside."

A gleam surfaced in Jono's gaze before quickly disappearing. "It was the strangest thing. He tracked me down here this morning. Said he had some more questions about Krista's disappearance. But I saw something different in his eyes. He realized the truth about me. That's when I knew I had to silence him."

"Where is he?" Michael sounded like he was speaking through clenched teeth.

"Don't you worry about that. I've got it all under control."

All under control? I didn't like the sound of that.

We were trapped down here with a madman.

How were we going to get out of this one?

My stomach sank as I realized we'd walked right into his trap.

———

"YOU SHOULD JUST LET US GO." I knew my words would do no good, but I figured I'd kick myself if I didn't try the last-minute plea.

"All of you need to get into a room. Now." Jono shoved his gun toward us.

"You don't want to do this," Michael said. "You're better than this."

"Of course I have to do this. I've been doing this for five years. Honing my craft. Becoming an expert in my field."

I stepped closer and shook my head. "Why?"

My timing might be awful, but I really wanted to know. His actions didn't make any sense to me. Not that murder always had a reason but . . . the pieces just didn't fit in my mind.

"I was never good enough for my family." Jono's nostrils flared as he said the words. "They pretty much resigned themselves to the fact that I was going to be a playboy. When I didn't live up to my dad's expectations, he beat me—it was his way of trying to knock some sense into me. It never worked. I needed to try to find something that I was good at."

"I'm sorry for what he did to you. But why take that out on innocent women?" The words left a sick taste in my mouth as they left my lips.

"These were women who didn't have anybody. It was really no big loss to anybody. And it wasn't horrible for them while they were with me. After a while, I grew bored of talking with them. That's when I knew I had to put them to rest."

"But you were playing games with the police," I said. "You picked those crime scenes on purpose."

He shrugged, a touch of pride entering his gaze. "People have never really thought that I was that smart. I needed to prove to them that I was. I'd say I succeeded. I've stumped some of the brightest people in the area and now the FBI."

I needed to keep him talking. The more time I could buy, the longer Michael and I had to figure out a way out of here.

In theory.

"So this is where you brought all of your victims?" I glanced around the space, which looked more like an upscale college dorm than a basement. "You came and went . . . let me guess? In a helicopter? That was a lie too, wasn't it?"

This man lied as easily as some people breathed. It was a concept I couldn't quite understand. I supposed that was why he was a killer, and I wasn't.

"My father loves his helicopter," Jono said. "I just couldn't let you know that. I didn't want to make things too easy. It's clear you're an overachiever."

As I'd heard him talking, a new plan formed in my mind. I knew it was risky. I knew it might not work.

But it was worth a shot.

"Jono, you can't kill us like this." I swallowed hard, trying to push down my nerves. "It doesn't fit your MO."

He stared at me for a minute, readjusting the grip on his gun. "What are you talking about?"

"You have a pattern that you've established." I continued to creep closer to him. "If you kill us, then that pattern is going to be broken. One day, when you end up in the history books and on news specials airing on TV, our deaths aren't going to fit."

His eyes wrinkled together as if he was confused. "That doesn't matter."

"But it does. I've been studying serial killers. You don't want to be known as the one who slipped up and killed extra people. It's sloppy. It's not going to fit the narrative that you're trying to establish."

I felt everyone's eyes on me. I knew this was a stretch. But I hoped the payoff was worth it.

"Then what do you suggest?" His gaze latched onto mine, as if he really wanted to hear what I had to say.

I stepped closer, my eyes still on his gun, which was beginning to drop lower. He had taken the bait. "Let us go."

Jono let out a chuckle, making it clear he thought I'd lost my mind. "That's not going to happen. You're smarter than that, Elliot."

"When we tell people that you're guilty, you can deny it," I told him. "We don't have any evidence to prove you're behind this."

"You have Velma." He practically spat the words out.

"She's drugged," I reminded him. "Her memories of us are going to be hazy. If you can move past the situation with us, then you are going to be ready to roll for a long time. Isn't that what you want? To leave a legacy of all the deaths you caused?"

"I just want my dad one day to know that I was good at something." Jono's nostrils flared.

"Then be good at it," I told him, trying to use my most inspirational tone. "Don't be sloppy."

He shook his head quickly, curtly. That's when I knew I was getting into his mind—just what I wanted.

"You don't know what you're talking about," Jono said. "You're just trying to get out of this alive."

"I'm trying to help you." I stopped in front of him. "You know what I'm good at? Details. They're my specialty. And I'm trying to offer you a little bit of insight right now. You're not paying enough attention to the details."

"Elliot . . ." Michael muttered behind me.

I hope he let me see this through to completion. I could feel that I was close. Really close.

"So I let you guys go, I clean up this place, and then I deny everything?" Jono stared at me, something shifting in his gaze. "You really think that that's going to work?"

"I think it could. You just have to make sure that no evidence is left here. I'm quite certain that you don't have any witnesses. The police would have found them by now if you did."

"What about when the police find out I have a helicopter?"

"A lot of people around here do. Certainly, you're not the only one."

"I just want my family to know that I was actually good at something. All I had to do was to set my mind to it." Jono's voice rose with each syllable.

"You *are* good at this. That's why I'm trying to help you."

Jono stared at me another moment, something softening in his eyes. "You're a smart woman, Elliot Ransom. I knew I liked you from the first moment that I saw you."

"I liked you too. That's why I was trying to get to know you. I've always seen something special inside you." My voice wavered, and I willed the shakiness to go away. I couldn't ruin this now.

"Maybe the two of us could even work together . . ."

I stepped closer, ignoring the bile rising in my throat. "I would like that."

As Jono stared at me, I knew I had to act.

Now.

I grabbed his gun and shoved the barrel away from us, toward the wall.

As soon as I touched him, Jono snapped out of his stupor. The spell I'd almost seemed to put him under had been broken.

He fought back, lunging toward me.

As he did, Michael sprang between us.

When he did, the gun fired.

I prayed I hadn't set us up for failure.

CHAPTER THIRTY-NINE

AS MICHAEL AND JONO WRESTLED, the gun flew out of Jono's hands. I dove toward it and grabbed it. Raising my shaky arms up, I pointed it toward Jono.

"Stop!" I yelled.

No one heard me over the grunts and yells from the fistfight.

"Stop!" I said louder.

Still, no one stopped.

I wasn't sure they would take me seriously with this gun trembling in my hand anyway.

Before I had to say it a third time, the door at the top of the stairway burst open.

"Freeze! FBI!"

Men in official FBI gear flooded down the stairway. One of them stopped near Velma and put a blanket around her shoulders. Shock seemed to be kicking in, and her eyes looked glazed.

The other agents rushed toward Jono. Michael had him pinned down. I handed the gun to one of the feds.

At the back of the pack, I spotted Hunter.

Once Jono had been officially arrested and Michael was on his feet, flinging his hand in the air as if it hurt, Hunter strode toward me.

"Good work," he said.

"How did you know we were here?" Jono obviously hadn't called him.

A shadow hooded his gaze. "The FBI asked me to plant a bug and tracker on you."

I gasped. "On me? Why?"

"They were suspicious because you kept finding clues. Personally, I think it was because they were insecure. They were just using the idea that you might be involved as an excuse."

"That's how you knew that Kiki was a receptionist up in New York . . ."

Hunter shrugged half-heartedly. "I accidentally let that slip, didn't I?"

"You had me wondering if you actually might be this Beltway Killer."

"It's always good to stay on your toes, Elliot—even if the results aren't what you want."

I didn't bother to ask what exactly that meant.

Instead, I watched as the FBI led Jono away. Michael went to Velma and murmured something softly toward her. The paramedics appeared at the top of the stairs.

Could all of this really be over?

"So you heard my conversation with Jono just now?" I clarified with Hunter.

"I did. I heard his confession. We were able to track your location. As much as I may have been ethically opposed to leaving that tracking device on you, it all worked out in the end."

"Where did you even put the tracker?"

"On the back of your phone," Hunter said.

"That day you knocked it out of my hand?"

He nodded.

I nudged the cover off and, sure enough, there was a small device there. I pulled it off and handed it back to Hunter.

That was probably how my phone had ended up getting turned to silent mode. That hadn't been because I'd put it in my pocket after all.

I was too relieved to be alive to be mad. Yes, it had violated my personal rights. But this time everything had worked out in the end.

"Can I get you anything?" Hunter studied my face.

I shook my head and glanced over at Velma and Michael. "I'm just glad that this is all over with."

"We all are."

AN HOUR LATER, I stood outside Jono's estate, watching as the FBI tromped in and out of the house carrying boxes of evidence. Velma had been taken to the hospital, and Oscar was going to meet her there.

I was still waiting to see how everything would unfold —because there were still a few threads that needed closure.

When Michael and I finally had a moment alone, he turned to me, reaching for my hand. "That was brilliant what you did back there. I wasn't sure for a while if it would work, but you managed to make it happen."

"I could tell Jono just wanted someone to understand him, to be on his side. Once I realized that, everything else made sense. I figured if I could get close enough to his gun, I might be able to get it away from him."

"It was still risky." Michael looked at me tenderly. "Something could have happened to you."

"But it didn't."

"Not this time. I don't want to see you get hurt, Elliot." His voice cracked with emotion.

Without saying anything else, he wrapped me in his arms. I didn't fuss. It felt good to have somebody to lean on. To be held by his strength. To know I mattered to him.

Because even though on the outside I might look strong, on the inside, I felt like a mess. A quivering mess.

Sometimes, I feared I might fall apart and never be able to be put back together.

Despite the tender moment between Michael and I, I knew that we still had some unresolved issues.

Before I could bring any of them up, someone cleared his throat behind us. I turned to see Hunter.

"Good news," he said. "We found Mr. Lawson. He was in another one of those rooms, and he'd been drugged."

"I think he has a heart condition," I told him. "Is he really okay?"

"The paramedics are checking him out now, but he appears to be fine."

"That's good news, at least. I guess Beasley was just another red herring that Jono set up for us?"

"So it appears. But his actions were that of a guilty man. He shouldn't have run."

"Did you find him?" Michael asked.

"As a matter of fact, we were able to track him down early this morning. He said he got nervous. Said he felt like he was being set up and that he didn't want to take the fall for this."

"What about the butler? Was he involved in this?" I asked.

"The man is claiming to be clueless. Apparently, he wasn't allowed downstairs, and he only works about six hours a day. It's within the realm of possibility that he didn't know anything. But we'll still be investigating, just to make sure."

"At least some of the victims' families will finally have closure." I tilted my head at Hunter, knowing that I was talking about him also. "I hope it helps."

His gaze locked on mine. "It does. It really does."

"Are we free to go?" Michael asked, snaking his arm around my waist and pulling me closer. "We've already been questioned and given our statements."

"I'll double-check, but I'm pretty sure you can. The FBI will be in contact if they have any more questions for you."

Leaving this place seemed like a great idea. More than anything, I wanted to put this investigation behind us.

But I knew there was still trouble waiting on the horizon.

Trouble that went by the name Roxy.

CHAPTER FORTY

"I'M GOING to go talk to Roxy," Michael told me once we were back in his minivan. "Will you go with me?"

I had to admit that I was surprised he wanted me present. But I wasn't complaining. "If you want me there, then yes."

"I've wanted you there all along," he said. "Never think that I didn't."

I didn't actually think that at all. I knew I was the one who'd pulled away, trying to give him space he'd never asked for. I still stood behind that decision.

If there had been any chance that Michael and Roxy were going to get back together and that the family would be reunited, I hadn't wanted to be in the way.

But knowing that Roxy had been lying changed things.

I reached over and took Michael's hand as we headed down the road. It felt good to feel like a team again. I'd made a lot of mistakes in my dating life, and I didn't want Michael to be one of them.

We were both quiet on the drive. I, for one, mentally replayed everything that had just happened. It still seemed surreal. But I was so glad that Velma was okay and that justice would finally be served.

I couldn't stop thinking about the fact that Jono was the one responsible for this. He'd so easily thrown Nolan Reid out of the boat and into turbulent waters, so to speak. He'd been right in front of me the whole time, and I just hadn't seen it. No one had.

Finally, we pulled up to Michael's house. We had a couple hours until Chloe got home from school, so the timing for talking to Roxy should work out perfectly.

Michael held firmly to my hand as we stepped into his house.

When we did, Roxy popped up from the couch.

Her gaze immediately went to our linked hands.

"Michael . . . I didn't expect you to be back so soon." A magazine rested on the couch beside her, as if she'd been enjoying a lazy afternoon at his place.

"Roxy, I'm going to get right to the point," Michael started, walking closer to her. His body language screamed no nonsense, all the way from his stiff jaw to his hard stare. "We know you don't have a brain tumor. Why did you come here?"

"Michael . . ." she practically stuttered. "Of course I do. Why would you say that?"

"You didn't go to treatment yesterday. You went to someone's house."

Her face went paler. "Why would I do that?"

"That's exactly what I want to know. What kind of game are you playing, Roxy? Why did you really come back here?"

She shrugged, still looking shaken, like a victim. "I told you. I'm a different person."

"I'm not so sure about that. You were never in drug rehab either. You were in Hollywood trying to make it big."

Her eyes narrowed, her shock turning into offense. "You investigated me?"

"It's only smart in circumstances like this. Especially when Chloe's involved."

"Chloe is my daughter. I love her."

Michael raised his chin. "So do I."

"I can't believe you're doubting me." Roxy shook her head and let out a long sigh as if we were the ones in the wrong.

As they talked, I turned away and did a quick search on my phone, another idea hitting me. I just needed to do some research first . . .

It was like I suspected.

Roxy hadn't met with someone named Terrence Smith.

Terrence Smith may have owned that house she'd gone to, but he'd made it available through a rental program.

Someone Roxy knew was obviously renting the place while they were in town . . . together.

"You're a con artist," I announced, turning back toward her.

Roxy's mouth dropped open. "Michael, are you going to let her talk to the mother of your child like that?"

Michael didn't even flinch as he looked at me. "Keep going, Elliot."

"You're out of money, so you came here hoping to milk Michael for some. You're smart enough that you didn't ask for it right away. But you were about to. Your treatments are getting to be expensive. You'll have a sob story to grab people's hearts."

"You don't know what you're talking about." She narrowed her eyes but didn't outright deny it.

"But I do. You came here with your boyfriend. You both needed money, and you concocted this scheme so you could get some. You don't care about Chloe. You never have. From the moment she was born, she was an inconvenience to you."

Roxy didn't say anything—which said plenty, in my opinion.

"Why don't we head on over to the house you're renting from Terrence Smith?" I continued. "With any luck, your boyfriend will be there soon. I'm sure he'll corroborate your story."

"Is all of that true, Roxy?" Michael stared at her, not letting her off the hook.

Roxy still stared at us defiantly. "I did find myself in a tight spot."

Michael let out a whoosh of breath. "Oh, Roxy. Even I didn't think you'd stoop this low."

"I was desperate. You don't know what that's like."

"I don't?" Michael's voice rose. "I was the one with a life-changing injury that took me out of the game I'd trained for my entire life. I had a new baby to care for—and I'd never even changed a diaper before. You don't think I know what desperate is?"

Roxy scowled again, looking more upset about being caught than she did her twisted motives. "This was just temporary."

"So you were going to leave Chloe?" Michael stared at her. "Even though you knew how heartbroken she would be?"

The defiance remained in her gaze. "Kids are resilient. Stuff like this makes them stronger."

"You're the lowest form of life, as far as I'm concerned. I took you into my home. I rearranged my schedule to help you. I almost lost the best person to ever happen to me. All because of lies." Michael pointed to the door. "Get out."

I didn't know what to dwell on more. The fact that Roxy had been kicked out or that Michael had just called me the best person to ever happen to him.

There would be time for both of those later.

With a huff, Roxy grabbed her purse and stormed toward the door. She paused before leaving. "Tell Chloe I love her."

"I'm not making any promises," Michael muttered.

As soon as Roxy was gone, he slammed the door and turned toward me. Tension radiated from him. "I can't believe I fell for all of that."

"You had your doubts. You just wanted what was best for your daughter."

"How am I going to explain this to Chloe?" Michael's eyes looked pained as he stared at me.

"She's a smart girl. It's going to hurt. There's no denying that. But maybe it's better that Roxy's true colors came out now instead of later."

"You're right." He let out another breath. "How about if you go with me to pick her up?"

"I'd love to." My spirits instantly brightened at the idea.

He took my hand. But, instead of going anywhere, he remained in place. I stepped back toward him, wondering what else he needed to say. I could tell by his gaze that there was more.

"Elliot, back when I was the good Christian boy that everyone expected me to be, I made a list of what my dream girl would look like. Once I left home, I strayed from that list. I dated everyone but that girl, and I learned some hard lessons along the way."

"What are you trying to say, Michael?" I had no idea what he was getting at.

He rubbed his lips together. "You're that dream girl, Elliot."

"Oh, Michael." If he was trying to woo me, it was working. I could practically feel my feet slipping from beneath me.

"I mean it. I don't want to lose you. I'm serious about this thing between us. I realize I almost blew it."

"You didn't almost blow it." I ran my hand across his jaw. "Sometimes you just have to find your footing in new relationships."

"Yes, you do." His eyes almost seemed otherworldly as he gazed at me.

I could stare into their depths all day. They were absolutely mesmerizing.

Just like Michael.

Without saying anything else, Michael leaned toward me and his lips met mine.

He may have been teaching me the skills on how to be a proper snoop. But, in reality, he'd given me so much more.

Coming Next: The Craft of Being Covert

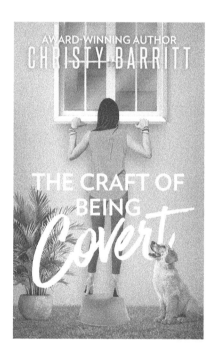

ALSO BY CHRISTY BARRITT:

THE WORST DETECTIVE EVER:

I'm not really a private detective. I just play one on TV.

Joey Darling, better known to the world as Raven Remington, detective extraordinaire, is trying to separate herself from her invincible alter ego. She played the spunky character for five years on the hit TV show *Relentless*, which catapulted her to fame and into the role of Hollywood's sweetheart. When her marriage falls apart, her finances dwindle to nothing, and her father disappears, Joey finds herself on the Outer Banks of North Carolina, trying to piece together her life away from the limelight. But as people continually mistake her for the character she played on TV, she's tasked with solving real life crimes . . . even though she's terrible at it.

ABOUT THE AUTHOR

USA Today has called Christy Barritt's books "scary, funny, passionate, and quirky."

Christy writes both mystery and romantic suspense novels that are clean with underlying messages of faith. Her books have won the Daphne du Maurier Award for Excellence in Suspense and Mystery, have been twice nominated for the Romantic Times Reviewers' Choice Award, and have finaled for both a Carol Award and Foreword Magazine's Book of the Year.

She is married to her Prince Charming, a man who thinks she's hilarious—but only when she's not trying to be. Christy is a self-proclaimed klutz, an avid music lover who's known for spontaneously bursting into song, and a road trip aficionado.

When she's not working or spending time with her family, she enjoys singing, playing the guitar, and exploring small, unsuspecting towns where people have no idea how accident-prone she is.

Find Christy online at:
www.christybarritt.com
www.facebook.com/christybarritt
www.twitter.com/cbarritt

Sign up for Christy's newsletter to get information on all of her latest releases here: **www.christybarritt.com/ newsletter-sign-up/**

If you enjoyed this book, please consider leaving a review.